# Lady Guadalupe of the Sno-Kone Hut

By Elvy Howard

COPYRIGHT © 2016 by Elvy Howard

All rights reserved. No part of this book may be used or reproduced in any manner whatsoever without written permission of the author except in the case of brief quotations embodied in critical articles or reviews.

Printed in the United States of America

Javier Augusto Reyes Sanchez - Illustrator

Bethany Orlowski - Hand Lettering and Graphic Design

This a work of fiction. Names, characters, places, and incidents either are the product of the author's imagination or are used fictitiously, and any resemblance to any actual persons living or dead, business establishments, events or locales, is entirely coincidental.

# Acknowledgments

First, I have to thank Angelica Swanson, my expert in all things Latino, and finder of the perfect Lady Guadalupe figurine, I love you, and appreciate your help. John McKee was generous with his time and gave much needed advice on boat motor repairs. My friend, Isabel Sturm, did exceptional line editing, twice, in the original version of Jolene's story.

And lastly, before I learned to walk, my father took us fishing. I thought all families got up before the crack of dawn, all kids thrown in the back of a station wagon in their pajamas, put in a boat and shushed the entire day because, "You're gonna scare the fish away." Despite this, he infected us with his love for anything having to do with being on the water, so I have to thank him, too.

Chapter One

It was soothing, was all, the way the tarot cards slipped together, sounding like rushing water as she shuffled. She liked the solid *thunk* of them on the battered, green-painted table, too. The sounds were the background music of her life and Jolene Gibson firmly believed a good shuffling did her as much good as it did the cards, righted whatever had gotten off kilter.

Old Mrs. Gunther's tarot reading caused the need for some righting. Jolene cut the cards with practiced hands. She'd given her home a sage cleaning after Mrs. Gunther and her daughter, Miss Ethel left, and it hadn't helped one bit. After a while at the table, she felt an ease inside take hold, and one deep breath later, allowed the sadness to leave. Notions of change circled her thoughts.

## Elvy Howard

How everyone and everything was always changing. She'd never lived one step from where she sat in all her forty-one years, yet knew enough to fill all the books in their little town's library. Magnolia, Virginia, by the Bacon River, fifteen miles from the North Carolina border, was all she ever required.

Grateful to get back to the world, she sighed and wrapped the cards in a gold silk scarf with long fringes, and placed them in their wooden box. Granny told her the box was made before she was born, from an apple tree growing on their property killed by lighting. Granny paid a wandering man to make it, and when winter's solstice came, she forced beeswax into every pore of that box and polished the hell out of it.

Jolene touched a tiny person carved into the side of the box. Men in pants and women in long skirts, bent and reached under the graceful branches of apple trees. In the slanting afternoon sun, they still gleamed from Granny's efforts.

Old Mrs. Gunther wanted to know if she should

## Lady Guadalupe and the Sno-Kone Hut

go through a bunch of things her doctor wanted her to try, or ease on out of this life. It was the way she put the question that made the answer bearable. *Ease on out of this life.* She knew Mrs. Gunther hoped for it, as much as Miss Ethel feared it. Each card in the reading said it different, of course, *lack of success if task undertaken, welcome ending to a long journey in sight, a new journey to prepare for,* and the message was clear.

She put the box back on its shelf, petting it like a beloved dog, and went out her kitchen, to the Bait & Tackle.

Responding to pounding on the front door, she shouted, "I'm coming." She tried to stop seeing the desperation in Miss Ethel's eyes as they'd gone out the same door.

Going through the store, she sighed, feeling the weight of a full day's work still ahead. A gurgle from the minnow tank reminded her to feed them before getting back to a busted boat motor and finish tearing it down. Yet before getting to minnows or motors, there would be groceries to sell, payments for trailer rentals to collect, and feuds between various Latino people to attend to. Everyone at the campground knew by ten o'clock it would be lights out and quiet, or she'd throw out whoever disrupted the peace.

Since Daddy died, the part of her worried *she'd* end up the Gibson that lost the Bait & Tackle had quieted down some, too, but man, she hauled ass to accomplish it.

She yelled, "Paren, ya voy," which meant, "I'm coming, quit yer knocking," as she neared the front of the store and unlocked the door. She took down the "Closed for Dinner" sign hanging in the upper, glassed-in part of the door, then opened it.

Standing on her porch was a group of very short, black-haired people – Mexicans, Columbians, Salvadorians and probably a few Incas from Peru. The men stood with hats in hands and shy expressions.

Their women entered first, smiling and not nearly as shy, murmuring, "*Señorita, Buenas tardes.*"

Lady Guadalupe and the Sno-Kone Hut

The kids came next, either very loud or completely silent depending on how long they'd been in America.

"Hey there, *Bruja*," said a grinning little boy named Mateo, looking directly into her eyes.

She tried not to adore the bold ones, at least in ways they would notice, but she smiled back anyway. "Hey there, Mateo."

*Bruja* is what they called her, mostly behind her back. It meant witch doctor, and Jolene took to the name, showing her pleasure to the ones who dared say it to her face. At least the Latino people seem to respect the title, unlike everyone in town who called her a slew of other names.

*Bruja*, it suited her.

## Chapter Two

A little after six, Leon's Jeep parked outside the front door. "I'm closing up for now." It was the same thing he said every evening when handing her a set of keys.

"How'd it go?" she asked.

Leon did the boat rentals, kept an eye on the gas pump at the end of the pier and with his son's help, maintained the grounds, boats, and trailers. "We did fair for a Thursday. Mr. Lewis took out one of the pontoons for most of the morning, did real well for himself too. Jackson got the ice box running again."

"Glad to hear that, I was hoping not to have to buy a new one right now." Jolene dropped the keys in the far left compartment of an antique cash register, trimmed

Lady Guadalupe and the Sno-Kone Hut in fancy gold curves.

"We'll hold up on the celebrating part." Leon adjusted his Mt. Zion baseball cap. "I want to make sure it's fixed good before getting more ice. I'll let you know tomorrow."

"Okay, anything else?" Jolene looked up, smiling at the man who'd been her father's best friend.

"Nothin' important. I put up the sign. There's only two fellers still out there, and they know to drop the keys in the box."

"The Gutierrez family is late. I don't know what's up with that. They've been good up till now, have you heard anything?"

"Naw, nothing 'bout them at all. Want me to have a word?"

Jolene hesitated. "No thanks, I'll, um, give them a few days."

"Okay, now, don't be forgetting Jackson will be running things in the morning while I take Lorraine up to Lawrenceville, right?"

"Yes sir, I'll remember. Tell Lorraine not to worry about it. Jackson does just fine."

Leon shook his head. "Not all the time he don't."

"So far he's doing just fine. You tell Lorraine I said so. How's she doing, anyway?"

His lips tightened before he spoke. "She doing alright, considering everything she's going through."

"Does it help?"

"The dialysis? Lord, child. She'd be dead without it, so yes. It helps a lot."

"Tell her I'll be by soon, for a visit."

"I'll do that and Jolene?" Leon said, touching the bill of his cap, his old face lighting up with a grin. "You take care now, you hear?"

"Yes sir, I will." Jolene went back to the twenty-five horsepower Evinrude boat motor clamped to the wooden counter. Parts were spread across newspapers, and the pleasant scent of motor oil was soothing in some way she couldn't name. The bell over the door rang out, as Leon left. The roar of his jeep faded.

Lady Guadalupe and the Sno-Kone Hut

Frogs in the river croaked, crickets and tree toads sang their songs, and an ancient radio on the counter played old country tunes, softly.

She had her evening beer next to her and was rebuilding the motor, checking its schematic, holding up various parts, before recognizing, among the parts scattered on the counter, a plug, which should have been replaced long before right then.

"Shit," she said to no one, for having to tear down the thing again.

The bell over the front door rang. On top of screwing up the repair, she was in a state of utter disgust at herself for being too damn lazy to lock up at six-thirty and allowing in what Granny called, "stray dogs." According to Granny, only stray dogs and people no one had any use for roamed around at night. But, surprise, surprise, if it wasn't Lyman Pettigrew.

"Hey there, Jolene." His Adam's apple bobbed up and down as he spoke.

Her disgust switched smoothly from herself to

the nervous man making his way to her. "Hey there, Lyman," she replied in a monotone, keeping her eyes focused on the Evinrude.

"Whatcha doing there?"

"What's it look like I'm doing?"

"Trying to make lunch?"

Jolene's opinion of Lyman was never very high, and in at that moment was reaching new lows. She asked blankly, "What can I help you with?"

His face fell, his eyes filled with concern. "Um." He looked around with a startled and desperate expression.

She wondered if he was trying to think up some new way to broach the subject, or was checking the store for customers. *Probably both*, she decided in the end. "What the hell do you want, Lyman?"

"Can I get a reading? You got the time there, Jolene?" He whispered, which was weird as crap in an empty store. But even more peculiar was him asking the question.

Lady Guadalupe and the Sno-Kone Hut

So unexpected in fact, it took a moment to decipher his meaning, When she got it was Lyman Pettigrew bent over her counter, asking for a reading, she was startled into saying, "I thought you didn't believe in shit like that."

Lyman bristled and spoke louder. "I never said that."

"You did too. You said you didn't believe in any of that witchy shit."

"Jolene." He smiled his banker's smile, the one she hated the most. "You know I never curse, so I couldn't have said that."

She hated the chuckle that followed, too. "You did, too, you bastard." She hesitated, unable to lie. "You said the part about not believing in witchy stuff." While pretending to work on the Evinrude, she pondered the notion of giving Lyman a reading and curious as hell why he was asking.

"Well, I meant, sometimes you say things that just aren't normal. That's what I meant." Lyman was quiet for way too long and only made it worse by adding, "You know you do."

"What in the hell do I say, Lyman, that's not normal?" Jolene slammed down a screwdriver and took a step back, folded her arms, and prepared to do battle.

He hated confrontation of any kind. It was apparent in how he arched his back, stretching his tall skinny self as if trying to somehow escape through the ceiling. She tapped her foot impatiently. *Why does he even come around since confrontation is mostly all he gets from me?*

Lyman gave in to the inevitability of arguing. She could tell when he dropped his shoulders, leaned over the counter again and whispered angrily, "You know that time you gave that woman a *love* charm."

He had no idea how stupid he looked. "Yeah? What about it? And why the hell are you whispering? Ain't nobody here, Lyman, but me and you."

He threw up his hands. "I don't want to argue. Is that okay? And besides, you can't change the way people

Lady Guadalupe and the Sno-Kone Hut

are, make them fall in love with just anyone. Nobody can."

"It wasn't a love charm like that, it was a love charm for *her*."

"What do you mean?"

"It was for her to let love into her life."

Lyman scratched his head, frowning. "Oh. What's the difference?"

"She wanted a love charm for a guy, but I explained it to her, my God, Lyman, *you* were there."

"I know." He sighed. "Still, how could a bundle of dried herbs and things change her life?"

"Because she would wear it, smell it and be reminded to be more loving, more open to love and kindness. That's what I told her it would do. You were there."

"Okay, I'll just say it, that stuff makes me uncomfortable."

"But a reading doesn't?"

Lyman pulled at the collar of his starched white

shirt, loosening his tie and running a hand through his blonde hair. "I guess not."

His answer irritated her no end, but she had the good business sense to cover it up. Sighing, she dropped her arms and resumed tearing apart the engine. "So you want a reading?" she sounded bored, disinterested.

"Yeah." He wiped his hands on khaki slacks.

"What for?" Hardly anything this fascinating had happened in a month of Sundays. For once, Lyman didn't have to worry about getting her attention.

"I need to find out something."

"Well then." She gave him her thousand-watt smile. Lyman relaxed. The hopeful look in his eyes was exactly like when he got to thinking she might be in the right mood. "I'd be happy to do that," she said.

"Do you have the time? Now?" Lyman, usually a passive sort, was uncharacteristically urgent.

*Why had she ever let this man in her bed?* She was almost sure the first time was a mercy fuck, what with him being drunk out of his mind and declaring his

Lady Guadalupe and the Sno-Kone Hut

undying love in the middle of the Bacon Bar and Grill. *But how do I keep justifying what's been going on since?* "It'll cost you forty bucks," she said. Which was ten dollars more than she usually charged and she waited to see if the tightwad would pony up, or try to argue her down.

"That's fine." He pulled a wallet from his back pocket faster than she'd ever seen. Two twenties appeared and slapped on the counter, next to a lone spark plug, the green bills sparkled.

Jolene's sideline of tarot readings, which had fed her more times than she cared to acknowledge, was also her pipeline to Magnolia and nearly everyone in it. For a female, she wasn't unusually curious. It was more something in her needing to know about the chronic alcoholic who'd joined AA and made it stick, who'd lost a job, or a business, who was sleeping with whom, or more often, worried their spouse was. She knew whose children were doing well and whose weren't. All the parts fit into an ever-changing picture of the town, and it soothed her, was all, to know what it looked like.

Like when Darlene Johnson's mother went unexpectedly nuts, as often happened in small Southern towns and instead of going to work at Pearlie's one morning, vanished. But Jolene knew who the mother was rumored to be sleeping with in February, and more rumors had her pregnant in March, and there was what was thought an abortion in April.

Darlene, a distraught fifteen-year-old at the time, had come by herself for a reading and it had been a good one. The cards said it was time to grow up, seek wisdom, and in the end, something lost would be returned. The girl's last card, about claiming hidden strength, had Darlene nodding her head as if agreeing with the steel filling her spine. Jolene had been so proud of the child, she'd hugged her and refused payment.

Occasionally a fisherman from out-of-town would stumble in asking about the sign advertising readings, but it was always the locals she treasured. And here was the big cheese himself, Lyman Pettigrew,

Lady Guadalupe and the Sno-Kone Hut

branch manager of the bank, waiting for a reading. No telling what secrets he'd spill.

"Okay, give me a chance to set up." She wiped her hands on a rag and went to the front door, set the lock and hung the "Closed Until Morning" sign her great-great-granddaddy made at the turn of the previous century.

His sideline had been sign-painting, and the stack of them in the corner still looked good with all his fancy red lettering. Gibson's Bait & Tackle had signs for everything, every holiday, even ones nobody celebrated anymore like, "Closed for May Day."

Jolene switched off the neon "open" sign and went back through the store and the drapes separating her home from the store. Lyman followed. Washing her hands at the kitchen sink, she told Lyman, standing in the middle of the room looking useless, to do the same.

Jolene's cards were older than the signs on the front door and looked it. Most of the backs were worn off and a lot of the fronts, but she knew each card as well as she did her own skin. They were thin and nearly as soft as old rags. "Now state your problem, or what you want an answer to." Granny had taught her how to make a big deal out of opening the silk scarf on the kitchen table and revealing the cards. He sat opposite, watching. Granny never made them state their reasons, but Jolene did, in service to both the reading and to her understanding of goings on in town.

Lyman was giving her the fish-eye stare he got when he was worried, or scared. "Whatever I say is sacred, right?"

"Sacred?" She laughed.

"Like a priest, or lawyer or something."

Jolene gave Lyman a hard look: the fool was bright red. "Blabbing everybody's business probably wouldn't be a real smart thing for me to be doing, now would it?"

"I suppose not." He was waiting for something more, maybe for her to come up with a better answer.

She sighed, like throwing in a towel. "Lyman,

## Lady Guadalupe and the Sno-Kone Hut

I never tell anyone's secrets. I never have, and I'm not gonna start now."

He sat and stared, the most stubborn man she'd ever known, an irritating mix of abject fear combined with a resolute inability to back down.

"How in the hell would I be able to stay in business if I went around telling people's secrets?" she yelled at him, which seemed to satisfy. She could tell by the way he relaxed his shoulders.

"I hadn't thought about it that way. I guess you couldn't."

"Of course not." She plucked the major arcane cards from the deck and spread them across the middle of the table. "The first thing you got to do is pick your signifier from one of them."

Lyman Pettigrew looked at the cards intently, just as if he knew what he was doing. He was only two years older than her, she'd known him her entire life, or known who he was, and his pretense didn't fool her one minute. Instead of slipping into irritation, like she usually did,

Jolene found herself noticing his silky blonde hair was getting thin on top. He must have brushed out all the hair spray he used in the mornings because he knew she hated it all slicked back.

As much as she knew he didn't have a freaking clue as to what he was supposed to be doing, she felt such a rare tenderness towards that pink, shining scalp, she got lost in the feeling.

Lyman asked, "What's a signifier?" He continued to scan the fading images of knights, pages, kings, and queens.

"It's the card you're drawn to. It represents you in the question," she said in an uncharacteristically soft voice.

Lyman looked in her eyes. "Which one should I pick?" The hopeful look was back on his face.

"The one you're drawn to?" All her softness vanished.

"I don't know which one I'm drawn to, you pick for me."

Lady Guadalupe and the Sno-Kone Hut

"Oh, for God's sake Lyman." She swept the cards up. "If you can't do the first damn thing, then I just don't know."

"No, don't do that. I'll pick one."

"Either do or go home." She gave him the narrow-eyed glare she used to let him know he was skating on thin ice and in danger of not seeing her bed for a while. "And you can forget about getting any money back. No refunds if you mess up again."

"Stop. I'll pick one. Honest. Please. Just put them back, all right?"

Granny's many warnings had been very clear, *don't never abuse the cards.* If you did, they would stop spilling their secrets. She had to be sure it wasn't only curiosity pulling her cart when she spread the signifier cards a second time. Spirit had to be there, too, which was a more elusive quarry. It was easy to believe it was around when it wasn't. She watched Lyman scan each card intently, his face hovering inches from the table. Jolene kept her face straight, even though deep down she was laughing, which was a good sign; spirits loved humor.

Finally, he made a selection and wordlessly handed it to her, his eyes wide and fearful.

"Okay," she said. "You've picked the Knight of Pentacles as your signifier."

"What does that mean?" His Adam's apple bobbed again.

He looked terrified, and she had a moment of feeling wonderfully superior. "It means you picked the Knight of Pentacles," she said, louder than intended.

"What does that tell you?"

"We'll get to that later. Let's finish this part first." She gathered the remaining cards and shuffled the deck three times.

Trying to hand the neatly stacked cards to Lyman, he ignored her outstretched hand. She shook them in his face. "Take the damn cards, Lyman."

He did.

"Now tell me what your question is.

Lady Guadalupe and the Sno-Kone Hut

"If I wanted to pursue something, how would I put it into a question?"

Her mouth opened, then snapped shut. She shook her head, knowing he was not that dense. In a monotone she pronounced, "You'd say, I'd like to *pursue,* and then fill in the blank by saying the thing you're after."

"I'd have to like, *name it*?"

"Yes Lyman, you'd have to like, name it." The last shreds of Jolene's patience were unravelling.

He sat, a tall, pale, lump.

"You have to name it and state your request three times," then, in what appeared as a stroke of brilliance, she added, "and every time say it different while shuffling the deck five times."

He began shuffling, slicing the cards with easy gentle movements. He had nice hands. They were always warm, warmer than plain old warm, almost hot.

He'd held her hand the whole time at the movies, but of course, that was in Richmond, so far away as to almost be a foreign land to both of them, where they'd been shy as newborn fawns with each other. He'd never take them out near home, where everyone knew them.

"I am pursuing a question of involving myself with the purchase of some property, with the intent of making some major changes in my life," he said with the solemnness of a surgeon announcing the death of his patient. Lyman cut the deck in half.

"Could you be murkier?" Jolene returned to the narrow-eyed stare, hoping to scare some truth out of him.

He smiled the one she hated, sort of snooty, yet smug at the same time. "I am pursuing some property and the option for a different life."

"Are you planning on starting a new business, quitting your job at the bank? The spirits need to have some idea what you're talking about."

"I'm planning on some big changes and want to know the outcome if I go ahead with my plans." His warm hands folded the cards together.

"Not clear enough. What sort of big changes?"

"If they're real spirits, they'll know."

Lady Guadalupe and the Sno-Kone Hut

Jolene wasn't sure how to argue his point. "You still have to say it three times."

"I already did."

"Well." He was right, and she searched her brain for another flash of genius, and found nothing. "As long as you're clear on what you're saying, maybe the spirits will be too." She counted the end of five shuffles. "But if this reading is unclear, don't blame me," she added grimly.

"I won't."

"Place the cards in the center of the scarf please." She'd been holding the signifier which, knowing Lyman the way she did, actually signified him fairly well. She held it up to face him. "You picked the Knight of Pentacles as your signifier. In nature, this would be as earth behaving as fire."

"Huh?"

She couldn't help it, she snapped, "Let me get through this before you begin asking a bunch of questions, all right?"

"Sure, Jolene. I didn't mean to disturb your thoughts or nothing."

"Earth behaving as fire means lava." He had better sense than to speak, but she waited a good measure before continuing. "Like lava, your signifier represents a force that is predictable, dependable, and also unstoppable. It's the voice of duty, honor and responsibility." Jolene stopped. Lyman appeared much too pleased by the news. "It signifies someone who is the opposite of an action hero."

"The what?" he gulped.

"In this question, you're like the opposite of an action hero, instead of using force," she slapped the back of one hand in the palm of the other, Lyman jumped satisfactorily, "you change the world with unrelenting, plodding perseverance." She made it sound worse than it was, with measured, staccato words and enjoyed the concern growing on his face.

"I have unrelenting, plodding perseverance?"

"I would say yes is the answer to that question."

Lady Guadalupe and the Sno-Kone Hut

He turned bright red. "Well, is that good or bad?"

"Nothing's good or bad, Lyman. Even if something sounded good, it could end up being something not in your favor with this *thing* you're pursuing. Understand?"

"Would I know?"

"Know what?"

"Know if something good wasn't in my favor?"

"If you'd let me finish this reading you might." She carefully picked up the top card, reversed it and placed it to the right of the deck. "This card represents the central issue of your question and is the Queen of Pentacles."

Not only did the Queen of Pentacles look like her, it was her signifier when she did a rare reading for herself, never more than once a year. If Lyman noticed any similarities though, he wasn't letting on.

"In nature," she continued, "this is the earth behaving as water, like a hot spring." For some unknown, stupid, stupid, stupid reason her face began burning. Luckily, Lyman was so focused on the card, he didn't appear to notice.

"The Queen of Pentacles gives shelter and comfort." Jolene's throat closed, and she had to cough before going on. In a gravelly voice, she continued. "And is steadfast, practical and domestic. Are you looking to buy a house or something?"

"Something like that."

"How's your mother gonna manage if you move out?"

"You know? There are a lot of things I might have to work out, but we'll just see, won't we?"

He could be such a damn snot, something she was acutely aware of, and there was no way to answer him, anyway. With a sigh of derision and a shake of her head, she took the second card and put it on top of the Queen, glad to be covering her up.

"This here is the Ace of Wands. It's an obstacle standing in the way, and when it's upside down like this, it means the beginning of a new crisis."

"Oh, crap."

Lady Guadalupe and the Sno-Kone Hut

She jerked her head. "Pardon?" It was the first time he'd come close to cursing.

"I'm sorry, the first cards were so accurate. I was hoping for more good news, but please, continue."

She looked deeply into his eyes. Sometimes an enforced intimacy encouraged the reading. "This card represents an upheaval of some kind. Something maybe not even known about yet, but something that will put momentous, even dangerous events into motion." There was no way to make it sound good.

He nodded his head. "Keep going."

She sighed, waved away an annoying fly, and took the next card. "The Six of Swords represents the goal of your question, and it's reversed."

"I can see it's upside down, what does that mean?"

"Are you trying to keep monotony in your life?"

"What?" His outrage filled the room.

Jolene leaned in and gave it right back. "Monotony, Lyman," she yelled. "Another name for this card is, *The Slough of Despondency.*"

"My God, what in the world are you talking about?"

"This card represents what will happen if the goal is achieved. Unless you are trying to achieve monotony, then this card is saying increased despondency will be the outcome, without some kind of a major change in what you think is important."

Lyman sat, apparently frozen.

"A reversed Slough of Despondency card signifies someone stuck in a problem because of conceit or pride."

The abject shock on his face made her reconsider, try and soften it. "You might need to look inside at things you're being too prideful about."

"The best that can happen is I end up stuck in some sort of bigger problem?" his voice went up an octave.

"Without any major change in your thinking, it does." So far, not a positive reading. She wished she had some idea what he wanted to do.

He took a deep breath. "Go on."

She shrugged and took another card. "Okay. This is the foundation or the reason for your question about whatever it is you are trying to do." She waited a full beat to see if he'd clarify the issue. He didn't.

"The Ten of Swords represents darkness before the dawn." Jolene paused a few beats more. "Getting close to the end of suffering through unexpected means, something that appeared to be a total loss holding the keys to some kind of success." She watched his head nod while he stared blankly into a space above her left shoulder.

"Do you understand?" she asked more sharply than intended.

He blinked, seeming to come back to the present. "Maybe, I don't know. Is that a good thing?"

"Good, bad, who knows? But it looks like your reason for doing whatever it is you're doing, is positive." She plucked another card. "This represents a passing influence on this question, something that once had importance but is now fading. Reversed, like this, means a valuable lesson from something unexpected that happened in the past." The man's blankness was irritating her no end. "You understand that Lyman?" she asked pointedly.

"A past lesson is prompting me to do this thing?"

"That's what it says."

"Could be, if the past lesson was about you." Lyman sighed.

Angry, she asked, "How in hell am I involved?"

"Because you showed me how to break out of my life." Lyman shrugged and glanced out the back door, looking every one of his forty-three years. "And I figured out how much I needed to do that."

She couldn't think of a thing to say and gazed in silence. Lyman's tall, sandy-haired self always seemed more boyish than manly, but right then, his age was showing. And it wasn't unattractive.

She shook her head. "Whatever, Lyman," she

## Lady Guadalupe and the Sno-Kone Hut

said and got the next card. "This is the coming influence around this question. The Four of Pentacles, upside-down like this, means using your power or influence to make someone's life better or happier, maybe even your own." Her eyes locked with his again. "This would mean a humongous change because it's about finding happiness outside of material possessions, especially money."

He didn't answer and got a stubborn set to his jaw. Jolene went on, angrily slapping down the next card. "This represents your role." It was a bad message, and she didn't know how to soften it, or even if she should. "It means any challenge met with force will be defeated. You will be tempted to use reason incorrectly." When their eyes met, she saw questions in his. "It's a card of corruption. Doing corrupt things, abuses of power, that sort of stuff."

He went pale. "That's my role?"

"Um, yeah, looks like." She felt oddly apologetic saying this, and wondered at it.

"Oh, — my."

She waited. It happened, sometimes, when the cards spoke to someone getting a reading, they'd spill the beans. She waited longer than usual, but evidently, Lyman didn't care to elaborate. She tried prompting him. "The best I can explain is at some point you will find yourself there, if not there already."

"Being corrupt?"

"Wanting to be, or abusing some power you have, or something like that."

"And that's my role? How I'm supposed to act?"

"Well, I think it says you will, and if you keep doing it, you will fail at whatever you are attempting. You'd have to change."

Lyman's face stayed pale. "I have to what? Stop being corrupt if I don't want to fail?"

Jolene shrugged and acted calmer than she felt. Everyone wanted the cards to say yes, or no and they never did. "I don't know. Maybe if you said more about it, I could translate. I'm just not real clear on what you're asking here."

Lady Guadalupe and the Sno-Kone Hut

"Is there more?"

"Yeah, there is." Jolene also wondered where the reading was taking them.

"Then, keep going."

She shrugged again and took the next card. Usually, with some finagling, she could get Lyman to do what she wanted. Not this time. Her curiosity was stirring, but showing it would only increase his obstinacy. "This represents the environment around the question." It was another bad card, and she didn't want to go on.

"What is it?"

"The Two of Wands reversed."

"I can see that. What does it mean?"

She sighed. "Decaying power."

"The environment is decaying power?"

"Yes."

He became even paler.

She worried he might pass out, or something. It happened twice before; clients so overwhelmed they fainted. "It's like a king or a kingdom, once proud, now weak, past its prime, past decisions causing current ruin, that sort of thing." She waited to see if he wanted to talk about it.

"Is there more to this thing?" Lyman sighed deeply.

"Two more cards." She considered taking him to bed after all, if only to make up for the reading.

"Let's finish it."

She looked at the next card before placing it, saying, "This represents your hopes and fears, or maybe indicates something unexpected."

He gasped when she placed The Hanged Man on the table.

"This isn't what it looks like," she said quickly. "It's not as bad as it looks. The Hanged Man symbolizes something new coming into play, and a firm letting go of the past. It's a powerful card, and depending on the change, holds the potential for great deeds.

"Oh, it's not like I'm going to be hanged, or anything?" The chuckle that followed was so empty, so

Lady Guadalupe and the Sno-Kone Hut
void of humor, it hurt to hear.

"No, no, of course not." She smiled, after this reading, he needed it.

"What does the last card represent?"

"The outcome."

"It will tell me what's going to happen?"

"In symbolic messages, yes."

"Go ahead." Lyman's jaw struck a resolute pose, like firmly turning down a loan.

Jolene felt his fear and her own. She turned over the last card. It was the Seven of Pentacles. She breathed a sigh of relief. "This says the outcome of all this will involve new work, or craftsmanship, maybe a new business, or a new set of skills." She sounded unreasonably happy.

"So, do I get what I want?"

"If you're looking at a new business, or something like that, you are." *Why wasn't he happier? This was one of the strangest readings I've done in a while. And, what sort of crap is he doing?*

Lyman sat across like someone hit in the head with a sledge-hammer. "What does the term symbolic message mean?" He was like a zombie, flat and emotionless.

She hated him then. Flat out hated him and his lifelessness. Between the Gunthers and Lyman, the day had gone on too long. A desire for him leave possessed her. She wanted to turn out the lights, turn on her bedroom's fan and lie naked on her high four poster bed until sleep claimed her, or all the bad feelings left. Lyman wasn't getting lucky in any way that day.

But, first a reading was owed. "It means you have to figure out what the cards are trying to tell you. I can suggest a ballpark of meanings, but without knowing any more about it, that's all I can do." Which was the truth, and there weren't nothing she could do about it. She focused her brain and shot silent, "*Go Home!*" messages at him, which sometimes worked on challenging clients.

Abruptly, he stood, knocking the chair backwards. "This is ridiculous."

Lady Guadalupe and the Sno-Kone Hut

"You're not getting your money back, Lyman, so you might as well go on home."

"I don't believe this."

She stared, watching him clench and unclench his fists. Once she'd been attacked by a client, but didn't have to worry about Lyman. Her eyes closed on their own. *I'm done with this,* went through her head.

Like a switch turning off, Lyman took a deep breath and let go of his anger.

She felt it happen, and heard him move closer, taking shuffling steps, and sensed him bend close then kiss the top of her head. She smelled the starch in his shirt, his clean aftershave and whatever good-smelling stuff his mother put in the laundry. He always smelled so damned good.

"Maybe I can come back around tomorrow night?" he asked, still leaning close.

She sighed, her hatred retreating to sadness. Sadness for the Gunthers, for herself and for the poor, messed-up man who said he loved her and kept it the biggest secret in town. She reached up and put her arms around his neck, pulling his face close. At that angle, they kissed awkwardly, but it was a sweet kiss. "Maybe, I don't know. Call me tomorrow, and I'll tell you then."

"All right." He kissed her cheek. "I will."

He sounded back to himself. She stood and walked him to the back door, to where he parked his car, always hidden from the road. She unlocked the door and opened it. "Call me around six," she said, knowing the moment he left, she'd get five sage leaves from their jar in the Hoosier cabinet, light them and give her home another good sage cleaning.

"Okay." He went out and stepped off the back stoop. He stopped, turning to face her, his eyes were level with hers. His look was uncomfortably intense and Jolene found herself growing wary.

"I wish I knew what it meant, the reading I mean. I wish I understood it better."

A dandelion seed floated towards him and attached itself to his silky blonde hair. She smiled. "If

## Lady Guadalupe and the Sno-Kone Hut

you ever trusted me enough to tell me what the reading is about, I might be able to help you make some sense of it. But, maybe not. I can't guarantee a thing. I could write it down for you, if you want." She'd carry the smoldering sage around the kitchen three times, that should be enough for a fresh start tomorrow.

"Yeah, that'd be great. Do that and I'll call tomorrow."

"It'd be another ten dollars."

He smiled, something he didn't normally do when associated with spending his money.

It was a warm evening in early September. Jolene knew after the sage cleaning, she would sleep deeply and not dream of a thing.

"Not a problem," he said. "I'll call tomorrow at six."

"Until then." With arms folded across her chest, Jolene watched the dust and gravel kick up around his tires, as he pulled away.

## Chapter Three

Mid-September in Magnolia was beautiful, with the soft warmth of the days and welcomed cool of evenings.

Magnolia had subdivisions, no fancy cul-de-sac contraptions, but simple grid-style neighborhoods. All built on farms sold for a shit-pile of money split among the happily surprised siblings who'd grown up on them.

Oddly placed among the still working farms, the subdivisions offered simple ranch-house communities, to middling Colonials and split-levels. Up where the river widened to a lake, someone built huge Mc-mansions on oddly small lots. She never went there anymore, favoring the small creeks she used to fish with her daddy.

No matter how humble, or grand, every evening

Lady Guadalupe and the Sno-Kone Hut

those houses bloomed with scents of meat roasting over briquettes, or gas grills with seasoned hickory.

The tantalizing odors drifted her way, sitting in a rocking chair on the small back porch off her bedroom, holding a Mason jar of Granny's tonic, and watching the sun slip down over the river. The scents irritated her no end. She resented the peace the moment was supposed to supply, being stolen by grilled meat and encroaching civilization.

She'd recently decided to give herself this time, hiring Jackson to work the store in the evenings. She took a sip, trying to appreciate the tang of rosemary Granny had pounded and steeped sometime before her death, ten years ago. The potion was good for just about anything female: cramps, headaches, childbirth, menopause, or when life handed you some new steaming pile of shit. Except none of those things were going on and she didn't have a clue what needed curing.

But, she was fairly suspicious *something* was requiring some sort of cure.

"Miz Gibson?"

Jackson had come around back. "Call me Jolene, please." She sighed. "What is it?"

"Yes ma'am, sorry 'bout that. You've got a lady friend up at the store, she's asking for you."

"Who is it?"

"Don't know. She got blonde hair." He hesitated. "I think she's about your age."

"Okay, thanks. I'll be right there."

Jackson ducked his head and ran back up the side of the building. Jolene shook her head, wondering if she'd ever get used to *this* Jackson. The little boy she'd watched grow up didn't appear to have a thing in common with the large man who'd just left. He'd been working part-time for over two months and *still* hadn't looked her straight in the eye.

Getting up, she set down the nearly full jar of green liquid and watched the empty rocker, rock. She pictured Granny settin' there, shelling beans or sometimes just settin'. That's what she called those times she'd stare

Lady Guadalupe and the Sno-Kone Hut off at the world beside their house.

When she was a youngster, she thought her granny quite odd for staring off at nothing. When asked, Granny said she was talking to the spirits.

Lately, it felt like she was beginning to understand. It would be a comfort to connect with spirit and wondered how Granny pulled it off. She stopped off at the bathroom, unchanged since it was built in nineteen-fifty-seven, and flicked on wall sconces screwed onto bead-board walls.

Her hair was a mess. Taking a few angry swipes at the mop of dark curls threaded with grey, she stuffed it into a ponytail clip. The stained T-shirt would have to do, she didn't have the energy to change.

Jackson was taking care of some last minute customers by the register. Jolene scanned the room, her gaze stopped by a woman standing next to one of the cream-painted wooden shelves. It was, of all people, LuAnn Rice.

Regretting the T-shirt, the old green shorts that

had been too big from day one, the hastily pulled together hair, Jolene went around the counter to her childhood classmate. "Hey, there, LuAnn."

"Hey, there, yourself." LuAnn greeted her with a hug, just as if they had been friends forever.

LuAnn had hugged her before, on those seldom occasions when they ran into each other in town, so Jolene wasn't thrown by the gesture. She awkwardly hugged LuAnn back. "What brings you down here this time of night?"

"I thought I'd just come down to see you. Isn't that a good enough reason?"

"Well, ….. sure thing, LuAnn, nice to see you, too." Not sure what else to say, Jolene felt the old sense of confusion come over her like a horrible old coat she never wanted.

Glancing at Jackson, Jolene knew, if asked, he'd say an old friend of hers had stopped by, *and he would be wrong, wrong, wrong.*

LuAnn stood, grinning, hands clasped, looking

Lady Guadalupe and the Sno-Kone Hut

exactly like the pretty girl she'd always been. LuAnn's slacks were ironed, as was the bright blue jacket she wore over a pristine white T-shirt made out of some kind of silky stuff. Jolene found herself longing for a silky top.

"You must be doing pretty well to be able to hire some help."

Jolene glanced at Jackson again. "That's Leon's son, Jackson. He does evenings for me is all."

"I heard he was out, so that's Jackson Booker."

"Yeah, that's him." She looked back at LuAnn, narrowing her eyes and trying to sort through the moment. "I can't remember you ever just stopping by before, LuAnn."

LuAnn had the presence of mind to look down at the scarred plank floor, blushing prettily and hesitating before saying, "I know, Jolene. It's something I'm sorry for, something I'm trying to rectify if I can."

Which left Jolene exactly where she had started off, no more clear about what was going on than a duck in the desert. "You don't need to rectify nothing, LuAnn.

You never did nothing to me, and I don't bear no grudges towards you."

"Do you suppose we could go somewhere and talk?"

*Maybe she wants a reading.* Jolene shrugged and said, "Sure." She turned and took LuAnn through the green and yellow striped drapes. Outside her kitchen, the sky was a bright, violent pink, with the trees turned black and dramatic. All of it disappearing with a flick of a light switch.

Jolene wished she could have watched it fade from her porch, undisturbed. "Can I get you something to drink? A beer or something?"

"Do you have any wine?"

"I've got a whole cooler of wine out front, what would you like?"

"Oh." LuAnn looked around the room as if trying to spot some wine. "Nothing. Thanks anyway. I, um..." LuAnn looked more and said softly, "This place hasn't changed one bit since I was a kid." She smiled, seeming

## Lady Guadalupe and the Sno-Kone Hut

to remember the green cabinets and dark wood counter tops. The same fabric that made up Jolene's doorway had been gathered by Granny and hung under the counters, hiding the shelves beneath. LuAnn stared at the Hoosier cabinet and the large, old, glass-fronted china press.

Jolene's classmate stood, going over and touching the walnut antique. "This is a nice piece. You might want to think about selling it."

"Where would I put all my stuff?"

LuAnn twirled. "My, gosh, Jolene, you could get a new kitchen for the price of this, didn't you know?"

She'd had offers, so had some idea. Jolene's real problem was trying to remember when LuAnn had ever been in her house. "Yeah, I just don't want to sell it. Wait a minute, let me get my drink in the other room." She went through her bedroom and grabbed the jar holding Granny's tonic. "I was setting out back, having some of Granny's tonic, when you came calling," she said, coming back in the kitchen.

LuAnn was back at the table, waiting. Jolene,

trying to guess what for, poured tonic in a small glass. She held up the jar. "Want some?"

LuAnn smiled. "I remember your granny's tonic. My mother kept a Mason jar of that stuff behind the spices. I'd forgotten all about it."

Jolene asked again, roughly, "Want some?" It always irritated her how the "ladies" of the town could never come out with a single straight answer to any question put to them.

"Yeah, I'll try it. If it was good enough for my momma, it's good enough for me."

Jolene poured a thimble's height in another small glass with cartoon characters on it.

Turning from the counter, she remembered the ill-fated, surprise third-grade birthday party Granny cooked up. Granny never knew, instead of adding friends to her life, she nailed shut the coffin lid on her granddaughter's social life.

She never did find out neither. Jolene convinced Granny she didn't like the kids in her class, she'd rather

Lady Guadalupe and the Sno-Kone Hut go fishing with Daddy, or hang out with the old-timers who sat up front nights, telling funny stories about everyone in town. That's where Jolene's picture of the town first got its start, listening to those old men.

She handed LuAnn the glass and put her feet under the battered kitchen table that'd seen generations of people named Gibson through some hard times. She recalled her classmates staring at the woodstove in the corner. Remembered them taking in the same scarred plank floors as out front, the old-fashioned gas stove and rounded refrigerator.

For her eighth birthday, Granny had set planks on sawhorses, making a large table on the screened-in back porch. She served the children a towering chocolate cake and had vanilla ice-cream soft for them. Granny's cakes were something to worship and Jolene's chocolate confection, sliced into big triangles with large scoops of home-churned, vanilla custard, was clearly appreciated by children used to little cakes sealed in plastic.

For a while, Jolene had dared hope it might be

enough for them to block out the rustic home and the stink of the fish house Daddy hadn't gotten around to cleaning out.

By the age of eight, she was able to differentiate between her father sober and not so sober. When he busted in the back door that night, looking rough as some lost hound dog they'd sometimes find on a river's bank, it was clear he was in a not sober state. He was wearing jeans and a red-plaid shirt that had seen better days. He hadn't shaved in a while, and a dark beard, grizzled with white framed his puzzled grin.

The clean, small faces, with cake and ice-cream in front of them, looked up in unison at the large man filling the doorway.

He found Jolene among them and cocked his head like a dog wrestling with some sort of confusion. "Oh yeah, it's yer birthday," he'd said. Her daddy, the most sought after guide for hunting, or fishing *anything*, was so overcome by shyness, he allowed Granny to lead him docilely away.

Lady Guadalupe and the Sno-Kone Hut

She knew it was those clean, mostly white faces, so unlike the swarthy colors of himself and his family that scared him. The store bought clothes not from yard sales, or whipped up on Granny's sewing machine, and the shiny, combed hair, or buzz cuts and braids, so unlike his family's own wild, unruly locks knocking him for a loop. She also knew not to hope for acceptance from her classmates.

Jolene felt a moment of sadness for her poor daddy, before knocking glasses with LuAnn.

"Not bad," LuAnn said. "Soothing to the throat, isn't it? So why wouldn't you want to sell that china press and get an entirely new, modern kitchen?"

"Um." Jolene looked around, wondering the same thing. "I guess 'cause it makes me feel my family is still here. If I changed it all around, I don't think I'd be able to feel them."

"That's right. All your people are gone now." LuAnn's eyes went soft.

Jolene had no idea what prompted her to say,

"Sometimes it's like I can still hear Daddy sitting up front with the old-timers, laughing. I went to sleep to that sound every night, and when it's real quiet, I remember it exactly."

"Well.... that's real nice, Jolene." LuAnn looked uncomfortable.

Jolene sat up straighter, angry with herself. "What can I help you with?" Jolene wasn't used to company, much less a classmate stirring up the past in such unsettling ways.

"I just wanted to visit for a while, see how you were getting along."

"How many kids you got now?" Jolene knew she had four children and the youngest boy was giving them a good run for their money.

"The same four I've had."

"Four, you say?" Jolene heard her daddy's words and mannerisms with people he had no time for. "Well now, that's gotta keep you busy."

LuAnn's face got a dreamy aspect to it. Jolene

Lady Guadalupe and the Sno-Kone Hut

figured the tonic might be kicking in. She stared at her old classmate. LuAnn had never been unkind, but Jolene sensed even in third grade what appeared to be kindness was more the excellent manners her mother insisted on.

Jolene knew good people. Women like the Gunthers, her granny, Miz Lorraine, men like her daddy, at least when he was sober, and Leon Booker.

She believed LuAnn was basically a fraud, except for the one time when LuAnn had taken it upon herself to try and help thirteen-year-old Jolene with her unruly hair. She figured it was pure pity that made LuAnn invite her over after school. She washed Jolene's hair, soaked it in conditioner she barely rinsed out, then combed through some flat beer and finally wrapped Jolene's locks around empty frozen orange juice cans, which, LuAnn insisted, was how she created her own shining, blonde tresses.

It had taken forever to dry, and when done, stuck out from Jolene's head like separate flat-headed snakes that no amount of brushing made come together.

LuAnn was royally pissed at Jolene's hair,

and Jolene walked home with her snake-bouncing hair feeling the same vague sense of shame that possessed her whenever she was away from home. Only that time worse, she realized, because she'd hoped LuAnn might've been able to pull it off – transform her into someone that fit in.

Jolene noticed time hadn't been kind to LuAnn's porcelain beauty. Her once flawless skin, never bothered by the eruptions Jolene suffered, had crow's feet around the eyes, the beginnings of puckering around the mouth. For the first time in her life, Jolene was grateful not to have LuAnn's complexion.

After a long pause, Jolene asked, "LuAnn?"

"What? Oh, sorry. Gosh, I'm more tired than I thought."

"Did you come to fix my hair?" Jolene grinned.

LuAnn tilted her head, reminding Jolene of a hound dog Granny named Bucket, for being as dumb as one.

LuAnn smiled back, saying with a shy grin, "Oh,

Lady Guadalupe and the Sno-Kone Hut

I think your hair fits you just fine now, Jolene."

"You do?" Surprise filled her voice.

"Yeah, you're the kind who sorta grows into their looks, I think."

*Maybe I've been wrong about her all these years.* The notion created an uncomfortable sense of confusion to reside in Jolene's mind.

LuAnn sat up straighter, took another sip and said, "I've got a ticket to a dance for you."

"You what?"

"My church is doing an outreach to all the single people in town and the dance is for anyone single."

"And you thought of me."

"You're still single, aren't you?"

"But I don't go to church."

"It's not going to church. It's going to a dance." She smiled like it was all settled.

"At your church."

"Yeah, it'll be fun."

"No, thanks. Besides I've got a boyfriend and

he's out-of-town."

"Who is it this time?"

Jolene glared, any confusion preceding the moment evaporating in the beat of a heart. But LuAnn didn't notice. She was busy looking around the kitchen, at the couch set up in the corner with probably the same quilt Granny had on it when Jolene was in third grade.

"He's not from around here. You don't know him."

"I know people outside of here, too."

"He lives in Carolina. He drives a truck." Jolene hoped that would satisfy her.

"Well, how nice for you. What's his name?"

"John Porter," popped from Jolene's mouth as if he'd been an actual, real person.

"Who does he drive for?" LuAnn was searching through her pocketbook and took out a small white envelope, from which she plucked a white card a little longer than a business card.

"Purdue." *Which was plausible, there were*

Lady Guadalupe and the Sno-Kone Hut
*always big Purdue semi's rolling the highways.*

"Well, bring him too." LuAnn sighed, drooping slightly. "Why don't you just think about it, give me an answer later?" LuAnn placed the card on the table and stood up. "I've got to be going. The youngest is getting tutored in math, and it will be time to pick him up soon."

Jolene didn't know what to do but follow LuAnn through the dark, empty store, unlock the front door and stand out front as LuAnn went to the black SUV she was so proud of.

After opening the door, she faced Jolene. "Why don't you come, Jolene? Me and some others from our class are planning the thing and will be there too. Why not give us all a chance to catch up with you? I know they'd like to see you."

*Fat chance that,* went through Jolene's head, pondering what her old classmates might be up to, but, "I'll think about it," is what she said, knowing full well her showing up was as likely as her going to France.

Jolene watched the SUV pull out, waved, but

instead of turning around and going back inside, stood in the light breeze bringing the scent of the river to her. Lights from trailers were softened by mist rising off the water. Spanish voices and music carried in the humid air.

She tried ignoring some urge growing in the pit of her stomach and turned as if it was a regular night with only a brief, unusual visit to separate it from other evenings. A visit gladly over with and nothing more. Standing on the porch, she watched a fictional self get created in her mind. Someone *normal*, who would go inside, brush her teeth, turn out the lights, undress, turn on the fan and go to bed.

But she only got as far as putting a hand on the screen door's handle, before longing overtook her and bent her double under its weight. Almost unable to catch her breath from the pain, a stifled howl escaped her lips.

She *starved* for the scent of anyone from her family and panicked at the impossibility of escaping the need. Possessed by a desire nearly impossible to bear, for someone too comfortable with themselves and with

## Lady Guadalupe and the Sno-Kone Hut

her. Even her ears hungered for the distinctive twang of her family's speech. All so strong, so overpowering, she didn't try to fight and so *strange*, she thought later on, after all the years alone, for it to come creeping up on her then.

There was nothing for it but go inside, close all the windows, wrap herself in Granny's quilt and bawl like the child she'd become. She fell asleep like a child too, soundly, there on the couch and waking up when the sun began to steal in.

A quick glance at the clock her daddy won in a poker game said she had ten minutes before opening the store – barely enough time to brush her teeth, change T-shirts and run a comb through her hair before putting it back in its ponytail clip. Even as she did those things, she was unable to completely wake up and operated in a haze.

The usual, small crowd waited outside the front doors. She went to the register, hoping to see Leon coming in soon. She needed his sharp eyes, as her own were barely able to keep up with the customers in front of her.

She sold cigarettes, collected rent, and dished up nachos and cheese. Leon Booker slipped inside and walked the front, keeping an eye on their customers. It seemed like the entire building sighed with relief at his presence. Even those probably getting ready to steal something, were a part of the sigh. Jolene felt like she was finally beginning to wake up and a second cup of coffee helped bring that along.

She thought about the night before, remembering the sting of grief and feeling echoes from it in her body. *It's not like I haven't been missing them since they left me,* and, wished again that Granny was around to talk to. Granny was always able to make sense of the things Jolene brought her. What would she have said about what happened in the night, on the front porch? What did it mean, that agony? She wasn't sure but studied on it as she helped her customers.

By nine in the morning, the store was empty.

## Lady Guadalupe and the Sno-Kone Hut

Leon was attending to whatever chores he'd assigned himself for the day, so she poured a third cup of coffee and attended to her own. As it was Friday, she entered receipts in the book, put down a week's worth of checks, inventoried the shelves, called the distributor and placed the day's order, but it all took longer than usual.

LuAnn's silky top kept popping up in her head, displacing figures, distracting her from bread loaf counts and taking her further and further from any advice Granny might have had long ago.

Mr. Gutierrez came in the store a little before noon. In halting English, he said, "Miz Gibson, I am late, I am knowing of this."

His eyes bulged with worry, deep folds collecting around them. "My wife had the tooth. It was infected and had to come out. They gave her pills, but it was much money."

A wallet, once leather, now rough hide and attached to a chain was pulled from his back pocket. "I have half last week's rent and will pay you in full next week with thirty more. In eight weeks it will be paid."

Jolene hesitated, she'd been burned more than once with families packing up and disappearing in the middle of the night. Always it started with some unexpected expense. But the Gutierrez family were good people, clean and polite. "How about sending me two of your kids to help out after school and homework, four hours work from each of them, for one day's rent?"

He had five children, and the oldest two boys were good, strong workers. Leon had been talking about re-doing the boat slips.

"Senorita Gibson," Mr. Gutierrez reached across the counter and shook Jolene's hand vigorously. "It is a wonderful idea." He grinned.

She smiled. Mr. Gutierrez left quickly as if to keep her from changing her mind. He waved, still grinning, before exiting the front door.

Jolene checked her calendar, she had three readings scheduled over the weekend, but none that afternoon, which she was glad to see. She wondered why. Usually, she looked forward to readings and idly wondered if her place needed another sage cleaning.

The clock struck one as Leon came in the front door. He placed the "Closed for Dinner" sign in the window and locked the door.

The balmy weather prompted Jolene to carry their meal to the back porch.

Gibson's Bait and Tackle sat on a rise overlooking a bend in the river. A driveway looped behind the building and beyond that, directly behind them, a mess of trees blocked the view of the river. When she had the money, Jolene planned to cut down those trees.

On the far left were the campsites with trailers of various colors and in countless states of repair. Jolene was constantly scouring used trailers for parts to scavenge or to replace the ones too worn out to be fixed. To the right she could see the roof of the fish house, high up on its stilts, with a floating dock and boat slips alongside. More river-front was visible, farther on, with a sandy beach area and beyond that was a huge ancient oak tree leaning over the water. All summer, children would swing from the tree on a thick rope, plunging themselves into the river. As the kids were all in school, she almost missed their shouts of joy. A meadow in need of mowing had picnic tables scattered about.

Jolene waited for Leon to bless the food, before telling him about the Gutierrez boys. "So, how much lumber will we need?"

"Don't rightly know. I'll measure it out after dinner and tell you then."

"Hey, Leon, what do you know about Mount Pleasant Church?" Jolene had tried sounding casual but failed.

Leon looked up from his plate, eyes narrowing as if trying to ferret out what she was after. After a pause, he said, "It's a Methodist church for white folks is all, no worse than the rest as far as I know. How come?"

"Oh, someone I went to school with gave me a ticket to a dance there."

"Sounds like a nice time, you should go." Leon

Lady Guadalupe and the Sno-Kone Hut took a bite of pork roast wedged in bread sliced from a new loaf. He served himself Cole-slaw and offered some to Jolene, who shook her head "no." The same happened with the succotash.

"Not with those stuck-up assholes, not me." She recalled the one school dance she'd attended, with a dress found at the thrift shop, cut down to fit.

But Granny's idea of what girls wore to dances dated back to the fifties, so the outfit she conjured up for her granddaughter was pure vintage and not at all cool – bright green velvet, with a wide, black belt to show off Jolene's waist. No couture seamstress could have better fit the dress to her ripening fifteen-year-old body.

Daddy, when she came from the bedroom she shared with Granny, was shocked. Granny whispered to her later on, it was because she looked so much like her momma. Jolene suspected it was more she'd somehow managed to grow up without him noticing, and felt sorry for him, while also real pleased at the recognition.

Daddy had driven her to the dance and when

dropping her off said as if angry, "Be right at this spot at exactly eleven o'clock and not one damn minute later. Got it?"

Jolene agreed, and went brimming with excitement but soon wondered what was so wrong with her no one asked her to dance. Why her few friends didn't seem to know what to make of her, barely acknowledging her presence. She wondered if it was her dress from another decade among the brightly sequined short dresses of her classmates spinning on the dance floor, causing the problem.

But in the girls' bathroom, seeing herself reflected back from the big mirror among the thirty, or so, primping girls, she knew it wasn't the dress; it was her. She looked like one of their teachers, an adult woman with a halo of dark brown curls, full-bodied and mature, standing among a bunch of skinny children.

She left out of there right after and found her daddy still in his truck, window cracked to let out cigarette smoke, with country music playing on the radio.

Lady Guadalupe and the Sno-Kone Hut

"What you doing here, sugar?" he'd asked, leaning across the seat to open the passenger door.

Jolene had gotten in, taken off the high heels hurting her feet and started crying. "Don't no one there got any use for me, Daddy."

"What do you mean, darling?"

"I got to quit school. I can't take it no more. Let me stay home and work with you, Granny and Lorraine. I'm ready."

He'd held her, on that cold night and said, "Okay, don't worry about it none, we can use you."

Jolene sighed with the memories. "You know, it was a good thing Daddy let me quit school when he did," she said, taking a bite of her sandwich.

Leon's eyebrows drew in, a puzzled expression again coming over his face. He slowly said, "I suppose it might've been when you think about it."

"Yeah." Jolene took a sip of ice-cold, sweet tea. "There's no way I would have been able to run this place if I'd of stayed in school. I wouldn't of known how."

"Lincoln died when you were, what, twenty?"

"No, barely eighteen."

"Eighteen, don't you say, well, my, my. That's been a while now, hasn't it?"

"Yes sir, it certainly has."

"Lorraine was still working with your Granny, then, wasn't she?"

"Yes sir and we needed her, too. Daddy's death hit Granny hard. I don't think she ever got over it, for real."

Leon sighed. "Lord, those were some tough times, I do remember."

They spoke of afternoon chores, of Jackson arriving at three and running the store, of Lorraine expecting Jolene to stop by later on. Leon brought up the subject of cleaning out the swimming area. "We can dredge it, bring in some more sand."

"But people are still using it."

"I don't mean now. Wait out the season, for sure. But we ain't gonna have us much of a season left if you

Lady Guadalupe and the Sno-Kone Hut don't keep them Mexican kids away on the weekends. I'm getting too many complaints, and they're ruining the business. If the weather holds, we got maybe another month of good swimming."

"I'll talk to them, see if we can't work something out."

"Okay, then." Leon slapped the picnic table and stood up saying, "That were a good dinner, and I thank you," same as he did every day. And every day he'd add, "Mind if I take some of that tea with me?"

Jolene laughed. "Not at all."

Leon filled a large Mason jar from the pitcher, placed his faded cap on his head, saluted and left out the porch door.

Jolene listened to the hum of motor boats on the water, of Leon starting up the lawnmower, crickets chirping, cicadas buzzing, all the sounds of summer, and not one of them giving a good damn what the calendar said. She sat in some sort of daze, not realizing it until her bottom began hurting from the hard bench.

Shaking her head, she put the dishes in the sink and the leftovers in the refrigerator. Instead of washing them, the dishes were left to soak. The clock told her it was a little after two and an urge to go shopping, find some decent clothes, possessed her.

*Maybe LuAnn's visit got me stirred up*, because thinking about what adorned her body was something she never had much time for. *Or maybe, I just need some time away from the Bait & Tackle, from the campground and readings, from problems and people always needing me for something.*

Jackson would be there by three. She probably should stick around so there'd be two of them to keep an eye on customers during the afternoon rush, but the notion of taking off an entire afternoon wouldn't budge. Besides, how much could they steal in one afternoon?

Mrs. Gunther died in her sleep, Wednesday last. The funeral was glorious, with singing and preaching like she remembered as a child. And, as a child, she'd sat in the same pew next to Miss Ethel. Seeing so many

Lady Guadalupe and the Sno-Kone Hut

folks from those days, all in one place again, had been wonderful.

Miss Ethel probably needed a visit about now. There was no way to call, as she didn't have a phone. Lorraine was expecting her later on. Lots of excuses for leaving early. Visit Ethel, do some shopping and visit with Lorraine.

Feeling if she didn't move quickly it wouldn't happen, Jolene wrote a note and taped it to the register. It told Jackson she was out, and to get his dad if any problems came up. She ran a comb through her hair and grabbed two jars of tonic

A sigh of relief accompanied buckling the seat belt in her truck. Jolene had two trucks and one was usually running fairly well. Her daddy's was an antique, with its wooden bed and fine for short trips. Driving east, past picked-out cotton fields, green fields of something coming in, she could have driven the route to Miss Ethel's blind.

She'd been Miss Ethel's pretend child. Every

Friday in Spring, Summer and early Fall, Miss Ethel would fetch her for the weekend. Back then, when campers, mostly fishermen, filled the campground, Granny and Lorraine had no time for her. On holidays, Memorial, July 4$^{th}$ and Labor Day, Lorraine even sent Jackson to the Gunthers.

Mrs. Gunther's father had built the home after the turn of the previous century, from roughhewn boards. Along with the house, he'd built an outhouse, a chicken coop, and a screened-in summer kitchen where they did their canning. A large, boxy, oil furnace dominating the living room was the only modern addition. A cast-iron wood-stove in the kitchen was over a hundred years old and on chilly evenings, bricks would be warmed in it, and wrapped in flannel, then placed under the covers at the foot of Jolene's bed.

The house always smelled of starched cotton, accomplished with heavy irons heated on the same wood stove. A quietness existed at the Gunthers that existed nowhere else in Jolene's world. It was made of gentle

Lady Guadalupe and the Sno-Kone Hut breezes coming through the woods, of chickens clucking and Mrs. Gunther humming some gospel tune.

The best quiet came at night, when oil lanterns cast their warmth and Miss Ethel read her bedtime story. She got them from the library, children's books with lovely stories. On Sunday mornings, Jolene would be popped into a starched, frilly cotton dress, given lacy socks and black patent leather shoes to wear to church. Miss Ethel would plait her hair so tight, it would last days.

Pulling into the dirt drive next to an ancient Cadillac, Jolene parked and got out. Miss Ethel was sitting in a chair on the front porch, fanning herself. She stood when she saw Jolene's truck.

"Thought I'd come for a visit."

Miss Ethel chuckled. "It's hardly been a week. I think I can make it *that* long."

"You think I'm checking up on you? Well, you'd be wrong. Big time wrong."

"I would, would I?"

Jolene went to the porch, "You know I'm not the sweet little girl you tried to make me into." She grinned.

"Well, now, I wouldn't know about that. Why don't you come up here and sit? I got some tea made, want some?"

"Crap."

"Pardon me?" Miss Ethel's eyebrows drew together in a way Jolene remembered well.

"Oh, I'm sorry. I meant, *darn,* I didn't think to bring ice. I can't believe I didn't. I'm sorry, Miss Ethel."

"Don't worry your pretty head about it. I'm used to the way we, I mean, I, drink it. I'll be right back."

"I brought you some of Granny's tonic, though. Thought it might be useful about now." She handed Miss Ethel a jar of green liquid.

"Well, thank you. I'm sure it will be nice to have."

Jolene sat in a metal chair from nineteen-fifty-two and enjoyed the bounce it continued to provide on its bent legs. Ethel pushed open the screen door with her hip, holding a plate of something in one hand and

Lady Guadalupe and the Sno-Kone Hut

two glasses of tea held together at the top with her other hand, letting the screen slam behind her.

She put a plate of sliced chocolate cake, pecan pie, and sugar cookies, on a table Jolene hoped was not as wobbly as it looked. With a sigh, Miss Ethel sat in the other chair. "I have to admit, it's nice to have you visitin' today. Right about now, this afternoon, I was feeling a sadness that was hard to contain. I was just praying about it when you pulled up."

She turned slightly and placed one brown hand on Jolene's tan arm. "I've been wanting to remember to thank you for Momma's last reading. It was a real comfort in the end." She shook her head. "So much going on, I could never remember to tell you before."

"Well, that's all right, Miss Ethel. I'm glad to hear it though. Seemed like it was hardest on you at the time."

"It was, it was." She nodded in agreement. "But I needed to face it and I got some peace about it before, before."

"I heard she was asleep."

Miss Ethel snorted, looking angry. "She was no more asleep than the man in the moon. I'd already told her I wanted to be with her when she passed. You know what she said?"

"What?"

"She told me she came into this world alone and I was done bossing her around. Like anyone ever bossed *her* into anything."

Jolene took a cookie. "So, how did she leave you?"

"We had oatmeal for breakfast, like she liked, set on the stove overnight, real low. She ate good and waited for me to make the trip to the mailbox for the paper. I know she waited, cause she got into her good nightgown, lay on the bed and had the covers pulled up just so, and that's how I found her, looking pretty as a picture." Tears slid down the woman's face. She wiped them angrily, with a rag hooked to the waistband of her dress. "Sorry, honey, don't seem like I can do much about it."

Lady Guadalupe and the Sno-Kone Hut

Jolene sat quiet, wondering what would be a comfort to Miss Ethel. She found herself talking about Miss Ethel's momma from when she was tiny, the ample lap, the bosom like pillows, being rocked on the same porch swinging next to them, moving gently in the breeze. Mrs. Gunther's humming, with random words thrown in. Jolene hummed a tune, inserting, "Jesus is my light," and resumed the tune.

Miss Ethel chuckled as she continued to cry. "She were a pistol. That's for sure."

"Your momma was an institution into and of, herself." Jolene wasn't sure what that meant. She'd overheard Pastor Cleveland say it, and it sounded right.

"Ain't it the truth, though." Miss Ethel pulled two forks from the pocket of her dress. "Don't know where my head is, anymore. Here, dig in, if I remember correctly, you like every one of these things."

"I will, if you do, too." Jolene attacked the pecan pie. "Mmmmm, good."

"I think Angeline Parker made that pie. I'll have

to look under the pan to see. I'm glad to have some help eating all this stuff." Miss Ethel took a half-hearted stab at the cake. "Momma told me some things about *you* before she passed."

"She did?" Jolene said around another bite of pie. "What?"

"She said you were too thin, something was wrong with you. She said a sadness was lurking around your door." It appeared to take effort for Miss Ethel to swallow her bite of cake. She took a sip of tepid tea. "Which meant she was concerned about you."

"Really?"

"No, Jolene, I made it up."

"Well." She was quiet, then blurted out, "She was right. I didn't know it then, though. Just last night. No warning, someone I used to know stopped by and after she left, I was torn to pieces. I stood on the front porch unable to walk from the pain of losing them."

"Your family." It was a statement, not a question.

"Yes, and looking back, for your momma, too.

## Lady Guadalupe and the Sno-Kone Hut

It was the past, all of it, all the people in it and how much I missed it – and them – how it used to be, with a desperation that scared me."

"I've had those moments when the past sneaks up and shows you the truth of how much you loved something and never knew it.

Jolene nodded her head. "That's exactly what it was like. I craved the past something awful."

Miss Ethel patted her hand. "I know exactly what that feels like. Once, gosh, it must have been more'n twenty years ago. I realized it was going to be just Momma and me, for the rest of our days. No more aunts or uncles stopping by. Cause they was all gone by then."

They rocked, sipping tea. "It passes. You'll find out there's more to life than grief. A good thing to remember right now. I thank you, Jolene."

"For what?"

"For reminding me of something I needed not to forget."

When Miss Ethel started yawning, Jolene knew it

was time to go and decided to do her shopping.

The half-hour's drive to Magnolia was consumed by thoughts of grief, exactly as Miss Ethel had described. Jolene wondered *when* it might pass and glad for the distraction of pulling up to the shopping center where Magnolia's only department store had existed for decades. A newer, chain store had opened nearby and people were betting on how long Pearlie's would be able to hold out against the competition.

Pearlie's had a long history of attempting elegance and the recent challenge to their dominion had caused the owners to spruce up even more. Jolene knew of the changes, but once inside, found the hushed tones of new carpeting, the dim lights, and soft music, unnerving. Even the predominantly female customers, either elderly or herding small children, were like natives from an exotic foreign land.

She left near as quick as she'd arrived.

It'd happened before – too much civilization for her to take all at once. She'd experienced the same

Lady Guadalupe and the Sno-Kone Hut

"crowded in" feeling many times and knew getting away was the only answer to it. But how to avoid civilization and still get new clothes, was something she couldn't figure out.

Miz Lorraine wouldn't be expecting her until later on, but since Lorraine rarely left home, Jolene couldn't see that it would matter if she got there early. The Booker's small house was on a pretty street lined with tall poplars. Their branches intertwined overhead and Jolene loved the cathedral-like feeling when driving there.

"Jolene Gibson, you are a sight for sore eyes. Just come on inside, right this minute." Lorraine, at the front door, was already turning, heading back to the den.

"I brought you some of Granny's tonic. Where should I put it?" The room felt closed in, too warm, with sunlight too harsh through the slatted blinds.

"Bring it in here, honey. That was mighty nice of you, Jolene." Lorraine was easing herself into a large plaid recliner. "Is there any sweetener in that stuff? Lord,

I can't remember the last time I had some."

"No ma'am, I don't believe so."

"Well, that's good. I don't want to be messing with the diabetes, but if this helps with those treatments I get, then I will be grateful to you. Lord, it's been so long, I don't even remember – how much should I take?" Lorraine, once a large, strong woman with a beautiful smile and one of the better cooks in the county, had been whittled down by cancer, diabetes, and assorted other ills to a much smaller person. Only her smile was unchanged.

"Granny used to have shot glasses. I don't know what became of them, so what I do is pour just enough to cover the bottom of a glass."

"Well go ahead and fetch me a glass from the kitchen. I swear I couldn't feel much worse than I do right now."

Jolene did as she was asked, pouring the green liquid into the bottom of a glass. She brought it to the living room.

Lorraine sniffed it. "Does it have alcohol in it?"

Lady Guadalupe and the Sno-Kone Hut

"Yes, ma'am. Each batch got a pint of grain, but those batches were big, Miz Lorraine, and Granny said it was only to prevent spoilage."

"What else is in here?"

"Oh." Jolene sat on the couch matching Lorraine's chair. "Rosemary is one ingredient. Lots of that, some thyme, sage, comfrey, mint, all those things she grew, you know, and stuff she collected, like sang."

Lorraine smiled. "Sang, you mean wild ginger, and I remember this smell, smells just like summer."

"Yes, ma'am, it does. Granny always said the wild plants she used were what gave it its strength, 'cause wild things were stronger."

Lorraine tilted the cup. "My, feels good to the throat, doesn't it?"

"Yes, ma'am, it does."

Jolene had a small bag of dried mint, rosemary and lavender in her pocket. She'd pulverized the leaves to dust and began taking pinches of the stuff, pushing them between the cushions of the couch, leaning over like she was picking up a newspaper to fold and put on the coffee table, but in fact dosing the far edges of the couch. She stood, taking the empty cup from Lorraine, and acting as if she was on the way to the kitchen, only stopping by the windows to adjust the Venetian blinds, so the glare reflected upwards, while actually spreading dust concocted to ward off gloomy thoughts.

*I should sleep in the stuff.*

Lorraine closed her eyes and rested her head on the back of the recliner. "Did you make this?"

"No ma'am, I did not, and I'm not likely to neither, 'cause there ain't no recipe for it. Granny left me about fifty jars of the stuff. I'd see them every now in then in the storeroom, but never gave them a second thought until a few weeks ago."

"Then it's an even more generous gift, Jolene, and I thank you. I miss your granny. She was a good friend. You know? When she passed, I realized I'd spent more time in that woman's company than any other person on the planet."

Lady Guadalupe and the Sno-Kone Hut

"Well, I guess so. How long did you work with her at the Bait & Tackle?"

"Over thirty years."

Jolene smiled. "And now Leon's taking over where you left off. Seems like us Gibsons can't never get shut of you Bookers."

"And us Bookers can't seem to get shut of you Gibsons, neither. Speaking of that, how's Jackson doing?" Lorraine grunted as she yanked on the lever that propped up her feet.

"He's doing real well, Miz Lorraine. I left him minding the place by himself. I think he'll handle it just fine."

"I got a sack of cukes, tomatoes, and zucchinis on the kitchen table for you, don't be forgetting them when you leave."

"Thank you, ma'am. I won't." Jolene stood in the doorway, collecting her thoughts about what needed to be said. "I'm feeling like you don't need to be worrying about Jackson so much. Honestly, ma'am, I wouldn't have given him the responsibility if I didn't think he could handle it. You know the business is all I got."

Jolene went to the kitchen and put the glass in the sink. Coming back to the living room, she pretended to gaze out the front picture window, while sprinkling dust. She knew it was important to get all four sides of the room. "Jackson takes his job seriously. I've worked with enough people to know."

"That's good to hear. I *do* worry about him."

"I think Jackson's doin' just fine. You need to be worrying about *you*, Miz Lorraine and let him figure out things for himself." Jolene went towards the fireplace.

Lorraine twisted in her chair. "What in the world are you doing, child, wandering around like that?"

"Oh," Jolene looked at the mantle. "Just looking at Jackson in all these pictures." She picked up a gold-framed photo of the family and turned to face Lorraine. "This is a nice one of y'all." Jolene sprinkled dust into the fireplace with the hand hidden behind her back.

Lorraine frowned. "That photo's been there

forever. Don't be acting like you haven't seen it a hundred times."

Jolene figured she'd have to get the last bit later, so sat back on the couch. The scent was subtle. Leon and Jackson wouldn't notice, they never had. Jolene worked her charm at least once a month, and each time sensed it lightening the house's load, less misery all around. "Anyway, that's what I wanted to say. Jackson's doing real good, and you need to worry about you and let him be an adult. 'Cause he is, you know."

"That's probably good advice, and when you're a mother, you can try telling me that again." Eyes closing, Lorraine chuckled.

"I don't think kids are in the cards for me."

Lorraine opened her eyes and looked into Jolene's. "I had a child late in life, so don't be thinking it can't happen."

"It's not likely, Miz Lorraine."

Lorraine's face went soft. "Is that a sadness for you, child?"

"Not really," Jolene answered truthfully. "I think Granny was right about me. I'm too contrary to keep a boyfriend, much less get me a husband and a child."

"Why, Jolene, you're not contrary at all. Why would she say such a thing?"

"Probably because it's true."

"In what way, may I ask, are you contrary?"

Jolene shrugged, uncomfortable with the question. "Oh, you know, like right before coming here. I was planning on getting me some new clothes and went to Pearlie's. I wasn't there two minutes before I found myself walking right back out the door again."

"How's that being contrary?"

"Well," Jolene searched for an answer. "It's like I think I want to do something and then find out I can't. It's confusing, is all."

Lorraine sat straighter, eyes alert and narrowing in concentration. "Why'd you change your mind?"

"I didn't change my mind. I need something decent to wear." Jolene gestured at the stained shorts she'd worn the past two days. "All my stuff is shot, but when I go in those places, it's like I can't take it."

"Take what?"

"Oh, how quiet and shiny a store is, or the fluorescent lights at the K-Mart. I can't stay there longer than five minutes without getting a headache."

Lorraine sat back in the chair and closed her eyes again. "That's not being contrary, that's a whole 'nother thing altogether."

"What is it?"

"There might be something to that fluorescent light thing. Even Pearlie's has fluorescents under some kind of covers in those ceilings. I read something about certain people being sensitive, like an allergy, to that kind of lighting."

"Really? An allergy?"

"Think so. Seems I read something about it."

"Maybe you're right."

"Your granny's tonic is real nice, Jolene." Lorraine looked half asleep.

"I think I'll be getting on back now, ma'am."

"Go by Mount Pleasant's thrift store. I bet you'll be fine there. I've been losing so much weight I'm buying all my clothes there so I don't end up running around nekkid. They got some nice stuff." Lorraine said softly, beginning to drift off.

"Is that the one next to the Piggly Wiggly?" Jolene asked, rising and getting the last part of the room dosed.

"No, it's downtown, in the old Woolworth's."

"I think I'll do that and let you get some rest."

"That's good and make sure you come see me again, soon. Don't be forgetting your vegetables in the kitchen."

"Yes, ma'am."

Jolene let herself out the front door, holding the paper bag in one arm and removing some sage from her other pocket. She ground it to dust with her fingers and sprinkled it on each side of the threshold before gently closing the door. It was a charm to prompt anyone

Lady Guadalupe and the Sno-Kone Hut entering the home to leave go of their burdens.

Chapter Four

Leaving Lorraine Booker's house with the feeling of having done some good, cheered Jolene up considerably. She took that good feeling with her to town, past the high school, the elementary school and the little park marking the beginning of downtown.

Magnolia had given up on revitalization. They'd schemed over the years to bring in new businesses by planting flowers in window boxes during the summer, parades at Christmas, and bringing different types of musical groups for some festival or another. All attempts failed miserably, and it seemed no one had the heart to try anymore.

The Woolworth was built in nineteen-thirty-seven. A brass plaque announcing this fact was attached

## Lady Guadalupe and the Sno-Kone Hut

to the bottom left corner of the building. The darker bricks above the double-glass doors still spelled out Woolworth, even though the business had left more than thirty years prior.

The building sat empty many years before someone had the idea to cut up the interior into different stores. The lunch counter still operated as a restaurant, serving the same food as had always been served there, hot-dogs, hamburgers, tuna-melts and vegetable plates. A section announcing itself as *The Antique Mall* held mostly old things, a couch that had seen better days, scuffed tables, sad chairs and lots of ashtrays.

Many businesses were tried, but only three stood the test of time – the fabric store along the left side, the restaurant in front and the thrift store taking up the back.

The Antique Mall had once been a used bookstore, a vitamin and herb shop, two separate attempts at a nail salon and other doomed businesses. People were betting on how long the Antique Mall was going to last.

Jolene looked at the large electric light fixtures in

the ceiling, wondering about Lorraine's allergy theory. She went in the thrift store, noticing her old fourth-grade teacher helping some customers at the register.

She smiled, glad not to feel the old jittery sensations. Maybe it was the musty odor of old clothing or the creaky wooden floors so scuffed they made lighter colored areas where traffic was heaviest, making her feel at home. She wasn't sure, but for whatever reason, she was fine.

The racks of clothes on skinny metal hangers mostly bent out of shape, held all sorts of things. Skirts were safety pinned to them, as were shorts. Pants were folded over the bars, stretching the hangers to oblong disks.

Jolene loaded up on shorts and jeans to try, with some T-shirts to go with them. Nearly everything fit and was so cheap she vowed to throw away all the stained, bleach spotted and baggy things she'd been wearing. When she got to the register, Mrs. Olsen was ringing up a woman who looked vaguely familiar. When it was

Lady Guadalupe and the Sno-Kone Hut

Jolene's turn, Mrs. Olsen adjusted her glasses and smiled. "Jolene Gibson, I do declare."

"Hey there, Mrs. Olsen." Her teacher's hair had gone grey, her body had smoothed itself into soft folds, but she still smelled like the perfume Jolene remembered from grade school. Jolene gave back a real smile. "It's great to see you." She began taking things from the cart.

Mrs. Olsen watched tan, thin arms piling clothes on the counter. "Why, I can't even remember the last time I saw you. How are you doing?"

It sounded like a honest question, and Mrs. Olsen's eyes were sparkling. Jolene was flattered no end. "Why, I'm busy as the dickens. I don't hardly ever have time to come to town, especially over the summer."

"Some friends of mine were out there for a reunion, now who was it?" Mrs. Olsen looked down, her brow furrowing, then snapped her fingers, a gesture Jolene remembered with fondness. "It was Macy Lee's people. She was telling me about how you've got it set up so nice, and how they really enjoyed themselves." Mrs.

Olsen sighed, beginning to ring up Jolene's purchases. "I was so glad to hear how well you're doing, Jolene."

"Thank you, ma'am."

Mrs. Olsen looked into Jolene's eyes. "You were always one of my favorites, did you know that?"

"I was?" Not sure what to say and feeling a bit uncomfortable, she stuttered, "I, um, had no idea, but it sure is nice to know. Thank you, ma'am."

"No thanks required, Jolene." She totaled up. "This comes to fifteen-seventy-five, with tax."

"Wow, that's great, I really needed some new stuff. Everything I got is worn out."

Mrs. Olsen smiled. "Everything you *have*." She took Jolene's money, gave change and started bagging the folded clothes. "Jolene, all you have here is casual clothes. Don't you need some dressier things too?"

"I don't think so. I don't hardly ever wear more than this kinda stuff."

"Not even some nice slacks and a pretty blouse?" Mrs. Olsen sighed, lifted the hinged counter and came

Lady Guadalupe and the Sno-Kone Hut

around. "Come on over here young lady, follow me." Mrs. Olsen went back to the racks of clothing, heels clicking authoritatively. "What are you wearing, an eight or ten?"

"Either, or. Depends on how it's made. I got to have room for these hips."

"You've always had a lovely figure, Jolene, no different now."

Mrs. Olsen's no-nonsense attitude helped Jolene accept the compliment. Between Miss Ethel, Miz Lorraine and Mrs. Olsen, she was reveling in attention from women that day, something that hardly ever happened.

It was easy to give in to Mrs. Olsen, go back to the dressing room and try on the things she brought her. Mrs. Olsen would hold up her selections and announce, "Now this would be good for a nice restaurant," or, "If you ever went to a church supper, or over a friend's house for a cookout, you'd look nice in that."

Jolene went along with the fictional activities

Mrs. Olsen assumed were part of her life. But, as she tried on black slacks with a shiny top, she began thinking it might not be a bad idea to dress up a little for when the picnic area was rented out for a wedding, say, or some family get-together. Who knew? Maybe Lyman would take her to Richmond again, and she'd surprise him by dressing like a girl, instead of the usual jeans, cowboy boots and soft blue work shirts she favored.

Jolene let Mrs. Olsen decide what looked best and before putting back on the soiled, baggy shorts she'd come in with, which looked so much worse by then in comparison, Mrs. Olsen said, "Wait a minute. I've got one more thing for you to try on."

Jolene stood in her mail-order underwear, which didn't look nearly as bad as her shorts and T-shirt, when Mrs. Olsen pulled back the dressing room's curtain and held up a dress, a deep red dress, with large black polka dots. Jolene reached out and touched it – some sort of lightweight silky stuff, but firm to the hand, crisp, not soft.

Lady Guadalupe and the Sno-Kone Hut

"We just got this. I unpacked it this morning. I think it would be perfect on you. Try it on." Mrs. Olsen was unzipping the back, unbuckling the wide patent leather belt.

Jolene did.

"Don't look, come on out here and see it in the big mirror." Mrs. Olsen grabbed her shoulders and turned her around, pushing her out of the dressing room.

Jolene gasped.

"I told you." Mrs. Olsen laughed with delight. "This would be fine for a cocktail party, or, wait a minute." She ran off and came back with a lacy black sweater. Jolene put it on, the sweater's high waist showed off her own narrow, black-belted one. "You could wear it to a wedding like that, or even a funeral."

Jolene turned around, admiring how it looked from all angles. She felt beautiful, and if she never wore it anywhere, she'd enjoy owning it. Something occurred to her. "What sort of shoes would you wear with this?"

"What size do you wear?"

"Seven."

"Give me a minute."

Mrs. Olsen came back with a few pairs of shiny black heels, but it was the spikes that pulled the outfit together, taking it to a whole different place. Jolene looked like a movie star. "I don't know as I could even walk in these."

"Try, see how it goes."

Jolene did and felt immediately elegant. A stateliness not required by flip-flops or cowboy boots was a necessity in those heels. She went slowly through the store. "I think I'll take 'em, Mrs. Olsen."

"You have to Jolene, I wouldn't let you walk out the door without them," Mrs. Olsen said with a wide smile and satisfied expression.

Jolene almost couldn't get home fast enough. She'd shower and throw out her old stuff, put the new

## Lady Guadalupe and the Sno-Kone Hut

things away in her dresser, or hang them in the closet. She wondered what she'd wear first and couldn't remember being so happy in a long, long time. Some part of her, lonely for Granny, had been soothed by those three sweet women no end. Her trip to town had started off poorly and ended up wonderful.

Pulling up to the Bait & Tackle, she took her bags around back, not wanting the store to interfere with the beautiful things and feelings she'd brought home. She went up the back stoop to her bedroom, showered and dressed in some chiffon flower-printed shorts, probably too delicate for everyday wear, but real pretty and light, with a lacy white top that set off her tan shoulders.

In the kitchen, she opened the refrigerator and pulled out some leftover potatoes and succotash to heat up. One of the tomatoes from Miz Lorraine was sliced, and a glass of ice tea poured. Her hair was loose, still drying, when she sat at the table to eat.

Her eyes lit on that white ticket as if it jumped off the table at her.

## Elvy Howard

Granny had trained Jolene to take notice of things speaking to a person. Like when wrestling with some problem and taking it for a walk in the woods, and a hickory knot might stand out. A knot from a tree long gone, yet still shining out at a person from a forest's floor. Jolene would pick it up, gaze at its smoothed out surfaces and understand the message: get tough, endure.

She picked up the card, turned it over and read the following day's date, seven-thirty as the time, Mount Pleasant Methodist Church as the place and did not want to think at all about what it meant.

But, it was impossible to miss. LuAnn's visit, the kindnesses of Miz Lorraine, Mrs. Olsen, all leading to a beautiful dress hanging in her closet and a ticket to a dance in her hand.

And she hadn't seen it coming at all. Granny always said spirit was sneaky and enjoyed playing tricks on folks.

Jolene ate slowly, one-handed, looking at the card in her left hand and thinking about the day and the

Lady Guadalupe and the Sno-Kone Hut storm of pain the night before.

Sounds from the store came in through the curtain. Leon stopping by at six and speaking to Jackson in low tones she couldn't make out, probably about her. But, she didn't move. She sat where she was, hoping with everything in her that Jackson and his dad might leave her be for one night.

Every time the curtain puffed from someone entering or exiting the store, she held her breath, but no head ever stuck itself through the curtain, no one called to her from the other side.

Jackson locked up at six-thirty, and she sat in the darkening kitchen, sighing and wondering if she had enough gumption to answer the challenge, while hearing an echo of Granny, somewhere, cackling.

## Chapter Five

At eight PM, the tires on Jolene's truck crunched the gravel of Mount Pleasant's parking lot. In that gravel, her spike heels made for slow going and only went slightly faster when reaching the sidewalk and the entrance to the social hall.

Fear, like a plague of locusts, had settled on her shoulders the entire day.

A DJ was playing a Springsteen song to which a few brave couples of varying ages were attempting to dance. The atmosphere was gloomier than a funeral and Jolene, hanging back in the doorway, felt sorry for any poor soul for whom the event might be the highlight of their week.

The Bacon Bar and Grill, across the river and

Lady Guadalupe and the Sno-Kone Hut

securely in North Carolina where she usually spent Saturday nights, was at least warm and friendly. The church's social hall, with light limited to dimmed wall sconces on dinged up paneling, felt as dead as a catfish left too long on a trotline – bleached out pale and a whole lot uglier than when alive.

She regretted being there with everything in her and was turning with enormous relief to make her getaway when LuAnn came up and grabbed her.

"Jolene, you look wonderful." LuAnn held her at arm's length, marveling at the taller, new and improved Jolene Gibson.

Jolene had gotten a last-minute, frantically made appointment with Betty Lou Stoppers, who had an illegal beauty salon in her basement. Betty Lou had said, "I've got Mrs. Smith coming in at five, maybe I could squeeze you in when she goes under the dryer. What do you need?"

"The works," Jolene had replied, surprising them both.

"Color, cut *and* makeup?" Betty Lou's astonishment was cut short as she admonished a customer, "Donna, get back under that dryer, you've still got twenty minutes."

Jolene arrived promptly at five and didn't leave until six-thirty to go home, get dressed and then go back to Betty Lou's for her comb-out and makeup.

Old Mrs. Smith got so interested in the whole process she hung around to see how things turned out. Betty Lou outdid herself; the before and after pictures thumbtacked to the wall proved it. Jolene's curls, shaped and tinted a deep, rich, dark brown, were shiny from some kind of stuff Betty Lou sprayed on when her hair was still wet. Jolene had bought two bottles.

"I can hardly believe it's you," LuAnn said, seeming to marvel at the arched brows Betty Lou iced down after waxing, to take away the redness.

"You look nice yourself, there." Jolene felt as awkward as she ever had and silently cursed the events causing her to feel so exposed among people she'd

Lady Guadalupe and the Sno-Kone Hut avoided most of her life.

"You come on with me now. There's some people I want you to see."

LuAnn kept a hand on Jolene's arm but had to slow her steps for Jolene's stately gait.

Lyman's eyes widened as they approached the group he was among.

"Hey there everyone." LuAnn's excitement was palpable. "Look what the cat dragged in, Jolene Gibson, all grown up."

Jolene forgot to be shy, she forgot about feeling awkward. She was too busy watching Lyman take in the transformation.

"Jolene, my God, you're beautiful." Then Lyman asked as if he'd never begged her to let him come over, "Where in the world have you been keeping yourself?"

Before she could think of an answer, Frank Paulson came up and grabbed her hand.

"Jolene, I haven't seen you in a long, long time."

She'd dated Frank a little after Daddy died. He'd

been fun for a while. "Hey there yourself, Frank. How's it going?" Jolene took back her hand.

"Better now that you're here. How about a dance?"

"I think you're still a married man, Frank."

"Not anymore."

He took her to the dance floor and held her tight as an old Righteous Brothers song played. Jolene was glad for the slow song and for Frank's bulk to hold onto as she tried to keep time in those shoes. He'd gotten beefy, almost fat, but was still a good dancer.

"I'd love to see you again, Jolene," Frank whispered in her ear, as he glided them to the soulful tune.

"I don't have much time to be dating, Frank. What happened to Tammy?" Jolene already knew, but was trying to keep Frank at bay by keeping him talking.

"Her mother died, she took the kids and moved back home."

"I'm so sorry."

Lady Guadalupe and the Sno-Kone Hut

But before she could say more, the song was over, and Billy Todd was asking for the next dance. Jolene found dancing in spike heels easier over time and before long she'd loosened up and was having fun. Between Frank, Billy and a younger guy who introduced himself as Mike, but Jolene didn't catch his last name, so didn't know who he belonged to, she danced for an hour straight.

She enjoyed watching Lyman Pettigrew watch her.

He would be trying to look like he wasn't, talking to some customers, or friends from high school, but she saw through the ruse and would laugh harder and smile brighter, with whomever she was with on the dance floor.

From the corner of her eye, Jolene saw desperation build in him and delighted in it. Lyman danced with some of his older, widowed depositors, always near the far windows where Jolene was. When he was standing on the sidelines with LuAnn, Connie, and their husbands, he would attempt to casually glance in Jolene's direction, in her polka-dotted dress and spike heels, dancing the electric slide, fox-trotting with Frank, or boogying with Billy. Lyman failed miserably, and he didn't look the least bit casual.

Lyman wasn't nearly as smooth a dancer as Frank, or as fun as Billy, whose jokes had her bent double at times, laughing. Lyman wasn't even as openly admiring as any of them, yet, still, when he tapped Billy on the shoulder to cut in, Jolene didn't mind. She didn't show it, but she was glad to feel those warm hands of his on her body.

"What are you doing here Jolene?" he whispered in her ear.

"Dancing, Lyman, what are *you* doing?"

He sighed. "I thought I'd be filling a civic duty, never expected to see you."

"Well, here I am." Jolene smiled at the end of the song and went over to the punch bowl.

Lyman followed, fixing her a cup, his fake banker's smile plastered on his face.

Lady Guadalupe and the Sno-Kone Hut

Their hands touched when he gave it to her. Jolene sometimes thought of his hands as attached to some other creature altogether, someone sensual, deeply caring and strong. Not the asshole in front of her, doing a poor, poor job of trying to appear as if he was only being polite to another bank customer.

"You two look like you're used to dancing together." Connie swooped in with her accomplice, LuAnn.

"Jolene just makes it look that way." Lyman turned to her. "You're a good dancer. I never knew that about you."

Which wasn't the truth, as Lyman spent just about every Saturday night at the Bacon Bar and Grill with her, so she didn't answer, only gave him a cool, narrow-eyed look.

"Yeah, Jolene, where did you learn to dance like that?" Connie asked.

*None of your business*, Connie being a person she'd never liked, one of the girls who'd gone out of her way to torment Jolene. "Oh, here and there," was what she said. Someone must have seen them, or their cars at the Grill. It had to happen sooner or later, something she'd told Lyman repeatedly.

"You never saw her dance before, Lyman," Connie's eyes turned to slits, "because Jolene here never went to any of our proms. Isn't that right, Jolene?"

"That's right, Connie. I was too busy working." She glared at Lyman, then LuAnn. "I suppose I'll be going on home now. It's been real nice, LuAnn, thanks for asking me."

Jolene turned, ignoring LuAnn's plea to stay and Connie, complaining, "What'd *I* say? I mean, what in the *world* is she upset about?"

Fetching her pocketbook from the table she'd pitched it to when Frank grabbed her, Jolene went steadily out the door of the social hall, far faster than when she came in.

Even the gravel was easier to negotiate. Jolene passed people gathered around a smoking stand, chatting,

Lady Guadalupe and the Sno-Kone Hut passed an elderly couple she didn't remember seeing at the dance and was almost to her truck before Lyman caught up and grabbed her arm.

"Wait a minute, please. What's the rush?" he asked.

"Careful there, Lyman, someone might think you know me."

"Jolene, don't you know everything I'm doing is for you? I'm trying my best to get to a point where it doesn't matter what people think. I won't have to care."

Which was as sincere as he'd ever been, and Jolene knew he didn't have a clue how insulting he was. "Let go of me." She shook off his hand. "Listen, I don't know why I came out here. I haven't done anything this stupid in a long, damn time and I'd appreciate it if you stayed away from me." She turned and went unwaveringly the rest of the distance to her truck.

"For how long?"

"For the foreseeable future." Jolene stood by the driver's door, swiping the shoes from her feet and throwing them through the open window. She got in, gunned her engine and roared away.

Lyman Pettigrew stood alone watching her drive away, looking like he was still trying to think of something else to say.

Mr. Atwater, the only self-professed atheist in the county, ran the Bait & Tackle Sunday mornings. He'd been doing it since Jolene was a child and even when times were tough, she'd never had the heart to let him go.

"Jolene, you up?"

"Yes sir, I am." She was sitting on the couch, eating cereal and watching TV when Mr. Atwater stuck his head through the curtain.

"Young man out here to see you," he said. Then coming through the curtain, he stood, rubbing his eyes. "It sounds like Jolene Gibson, but as I live and breathe, I

Lady Guadalupe and the Sno-Kone Hut don't think it's her."

Jolene laughed. As she'd brushed her teeth that morning, her reflection in the mirror had startled her too.

"Looking good there, young lady," He nodded and ducked out the curtain before Jolene could ask who it was.

To Mr. Atwater, a young man could mean anything from a child to a sixty-some years old. Jolene sighed, brushed cereal crumbs off her T-shirt and went out.

This time Mr. Atwater was right, it *was* a young man, a sixteen-year-old resident of her trailer park called Scotty, of all things, which must have been his English translation for Salvador, or something.

"Hey there, Miz Gibson." He held a battered, faded navy baseball cap in his hands. "I was wondering if you had any work needing doing."

He'd probably heard about the Gutierrez boys getting work and was hoping to get on board for pay, but Jolene had another idea.

"Well, Scotty, there isn't much I need right now." Jolene watched him deflate for a moment. "Except for one thing, although I'm not sure you'd be interested."

"I'd be interested, tell me, what is it?"

"I've been thinking about the swimming area."

"What about it."

"I was thinking about paying someone to keep the kids away on the weekends, but I'd let you-all use it Monday through Thursday, as much as you like in exchange."

"For free?"

"Yeah." Leon wouldn't miss having to collect the dollar a day swimming fee from children who all looked to him like the same damned olive skinned, black-headed child.

Scotty asked, "How would this person keep the kids away?"

"He would have to pay off the kids who wouldn't obey. He'd have to know who these people were and hire them, I think."

Lady Guadalupe and the Sno-Kone Hut

"Hire them?"

"Yeah, make them his deputies to enforce the rule."

"How much would this man be able to pay them?

"I'd give this man," Jolene smiled at the short boy in front of her. "I'd give him fifty dollars a week for him and his crew."

She watched him calculating how much he'd have to dole out, how much he could keep. "I could do that."

"You sure?"

"Yes, ma'am." He grinned.

"If anyone messes up, the deal is off. Understand?"

"Si. Yes."

"Okay then, it starts today. Come with me."

Scotty followed her to her kitchen, where she turned off the TV and unlocked the desk. Jolene pulled out her checkbook for the business and wrote a check for fifty dollars, asking Scotty to spell his name, which turned out to be Santino Vicente. She tore it from the book and handed it to him. "You can take this out front and cash it."

"Yes ma'am, thank you, ma'am."

"Everything goes okay between now and next Sunday, you come back here for another check. Understand?"

"Si, Miz Gibson, gracias."

"Beginning today, right? And the job is over when it gets too cold to swim, okay?"

"Si, I am beginning work right now." Scotty grinned again and left.

Jolene sighed, hoping the revival scheduled for the afternoon would go better, with one concern fixed.

She sat on the couch and was picking up her bowl of cereal again when the back door opened. "Jolene, I've got to talk to you."

She glared. "You know, Lyman, it's broad daylight out there, someone's bound to see you." She lifted the spoon to her lips and with a mouth full of cereal, said, "People walking around all over the place and don't be

Lady Guadalupe and the Sno-Kone Hut

thinking those Mexicans don't gossip either." She waved the spoon. "Plus, Mr. Atwater's hearing is perfect, and he's," using the spoon she jabbed towards the curtain, "right out there."

Lyman threw up his hands, bent over and whispered, "Will you please keep your voice down?"

Jolene stood and went towards him, yelling, "Will you leave, I mean leave right now? I told you to stay away, remember?"

They stood glaring at each other, each unwilling to give in. The clock bonged the hour, startling them, then resumed ticking.

Lyman's shoulders dropped, and he stared at the floor, defeat leaking from him like a sieve.

When he looked up, Jolene noticed how bloodshot his eyes were and how his blue eyes looked so much bluer. "For God's sake, Jolene," he said hoarsely.

She realized he hadn't been whispering. He'd been hurting something awful, so bad he could hardly speak. "What in the hell happened to you?" she asked.

"You get drunk or something?"

Lyman rubbed the back of his neck. He wore old jeans, and a pink, rumpled polo shirt. "Something like that. Mind if I sit down?"

"Go ahead." Jolene nodded, exactly as if they hadn't been like two snarling dogs a moment before.

Lyman did, with a groan and leaned back against the quilt, closing his eyes. "I thought you might have gone to the Bacon last night, so I did too."

Jolene hadn't moved. She stood in the middle of the kitchen with her arms crossed. "Well, I wasn't there."

"I know."

"What happened?"

"I got in a fight."

"A fight?"

"Yeah."

"With who?"

"I don't know his name, that guy with the ponytail."

"What over?" There were lots of ponytailed guys

Lady Guadalupe and the Sno-Kone Hut at the Bacon.

"I'm not sure. I was pretty drunk by then. It wasn't much of a fight." Lyman opened his eyes, staring at the ceiling. "They took away my keys. I had to sleep in my car and wait for them to come back so I could leave."

Jolene laughed. "They did that to me once, too, made me re-think my drinking some. But I've got something will help." She went in the pantry and got a jar of tonic. "This'll help." She poured the green liquid into the bottom of a coffee cup, poured a second glass full of water and brought them to the couch. "Drink this." She handed the water to Lyman. "Drink it all. You need it."

When he was done, she traded him for the coffee cup of tonic and put the empty glass in the sink.

Lyman watched her. He smiled. "You still look real nice, Jolene, real nice." He sipped the tonic. Leaning back and closing his eyes again, he said, "Doesn't taste bad at all, you got any aspirin?"

"I think you'd better be eating something first." Jolene was surprised at how calm he was, with none of his nervous gestures to annoy her. *Maybe he's too sick to get worked up.*

Lyman groaned. "Not yet, please. Come on back over here, I miss you," he said, not sounding like himself at all.

Jolene sat on the far edge of the couch. Lyman leaned over and grabbed her hand. "I am so sorry about last night."

Jolene didn't say anything. She didn't snatch her hand away, either.

"I know you think I'm ashamed of you, or something." He sat up, took another sip, then rested his head back on the couch and turned towards her. "I'm not ashamed of you one iota, not one tiny bit."

"Sure didn't look that way." She folded her arms over her chest again. "And you know the whole thing was a God-damned set-up anyway, by all your so-called friends."

Lyman groaned again, rubbing his face, "I know, I know, but all I can hope is if we don't act like it's true,

Lady Guadalupe and the Sno-Kone Hut then there's nothing anyone can say, for real."

"Jesus Christ, Lyman." Jolene started to stand up, but Lyman grabbed her arm quicker than she would have believed him capable.

"My God, Jolene, any man in the room would have been proud to be with you last night."

"So why weren't you? What's the damn problem?"

Lyman sat up, drained the cup and placed it on the steamer trunk Jolene used as a coffee table. "Remember when Myrna and I were going together?"

Jolene nodded. It was around when Granny died.

"We dated for three years. I can't tell you how awful it was." He bent over and put his head in his hands. "Horrible. Those women had us married almost from the get-go and were always asking me when I was gonna make an honest woman of her."

He sat up, those blue eyes looking into Jolene's. "The guys were worse, always trying to find out how Myrna was in the sack, asking if she gave me blow jobs," he shook his head, "stuff like that. Can you imagine what my life would turn into if they knew I was dating you?" Lyman shook his head again.

"I liked Myrna fine." He paused. "It's just..." Lyman's eyes glazed over then cleared. "I never loved her. I knew we were only two people who didn't fight. We weren't two people who loved or even enjoyed each other, and it wasn't enough."

"So you didn't marry her, so what?"

"It was the hardest thing I've ever done." He stood, carrying the cup to the sink and rinsing it out before placing it in the dish drainer. He turned. "Some of her friends cancelled long standing accounts with us, but that was only the beginning. Even my mother started asking me why I'd broken it off with that poor, poor Myrna." He ran his hand through his uncombed hair. "I knew it would be that way, too. I dated her for a year longer than I wanted to, trying to figure out a way to end it."

"Your friends wouldn't care if you broke up with

me."

"I know. Wait a minute." He shook his hands like a traffic cop. "Now don't go getting all riled up, I didn't mean it that way. It's just I know I'd start hearing stuff like, Myrna wasn't good enough for you, but Jolene Gibson is? Everything would get all stirred up again."

"Lyman, do you have any notion of how insulting that is?"

"I don't mean it that way at all. It's never what *I* would say, and you know it." He came back to the couch and sat.

Jolene scooted away. "It's like Myrna McCoy is so fucking superior to a low-life like me."

Lyman winced like he always did when she swore. "It's not like that for me. You have to know it isn't. But it's what they'd say, and that would get Myrna worked up all over again, talking about how she wasted her life on me. Me; the great tragedy of her life and I only dated the woman for three years. I wish she'd found herself someone else to marry before now." Lyman stared at a knot in a floorboard.

He looked exhausted. Jolene resisted an urge to pity. "So all the acting like you didn't know me was to keep Myrna from singing the blues?" She waited for an answer.

"Mostly." Lyman raised his eyes to hers. She noticed they were no longer so bloodshot.

"What's the rest of it?'

"Don't you know I love you, Jolene? God knows I tell you often enough."

"Yeah, but what's the rest of it?"

Jolene watched the tonic's gentleness take over. Lyman relaxed back on the couch, his shoulders dropping and he twisted his head from side-to-side, cracking his neck and smiling a slow smile with a lot of sadness in it.

"The rest of it is, I'm not a good fighter."

"I know you don't like to fight, Lyman." His lack of a response, whenever she argued with him, was her most frequent complaint.

"I mean fist fight, like last night."

Lady Guadalupe and the Sno-Kone Hut

"What in the hell does that have to do with me?"

"It was about you."

"I thought you couldn't remember."

"I remember that much."

"What happened?"

"That guy with the long, grey ponytail, the old dude who sits under the deer heads."

In her mind's eye, she scanned the long, scarred bar on a typical Saturday night, looking for a ponytail. "Jesse Forfever? That old coot?"

"Jesse." Lyman looked down again. "Yeah, I think so."

"What about him?"

Lyman leaned back into the couch with his hands on his stomach and, closing his eyes, said in a country twang, "How's that Jolene treating you there, bud? I bet she gives you a good run for your money. I heard she were some kinda wildcat in the bedroom."

Which sounded so much like Jesse, Jolene didn't say anything at all, just blushed.

Lyman opened his eyes. "Do you have any idea how long I loved you before I said anything?"

Jolene looked at the same knot in the floorboard Lyman had been considering earlier. "You told me."

"You were the last person I ever expected to feel this way about, but I do. To me, you are like some kind of wild creature, and even though I never know what to expect next, so help me God, I can't help it, I love you." His words drifted off as he closed his eyes again.

The tonic had him completely, his face as empty as an infant's. She stood and went to her bedroom, grabbing her sheet and a pillow. She placed the pillow on the couch and pushed Lyman's head to it, covering him with the sheet. He didn't resist, only kicked off his loafers and pulled his narrow bare feet up. Jolene switched on the ceiling fan. It was loud and would block out store's sounds. Lyman didn't move. His skinny self was stretched out on her couch, his silky blonde hair falling over his closed eyes and oblivious to the world.

One naked foot stuck from under the sheet,

Lady Guadalupe and the Sno-Kone Hut

exposed to the breeze from the fan overhead and Lyman Pettigrew, branch manager of the First Citizens Bank of Magnolia, was transformed into an elongated version of the boy he'd once been. Jolene remembered that tall shining boy, leaping to catch a baseball, not caring if he bashed into a fence, only focused on that ball.

She also recalled the girl she was then and how that same boy gave her a first-ever, heart-stopping moment.

## Chapter Six

The relative coolness of the Bait & Tackle, as Jolene slid through the curtains, was welcome. As was getting away from Lyman and the disturbing memories he stirred up, and more disturbing things he said.

"Hey there, Mr. Atwater."

Before Mr. Atwater could reply, Jolene was confronted with the uncomfortable notion she'd have to find out what he knew about Lyman's presence in her home. Mr. Atwater was bound to have heard something, and if he knew it was Lyman Pettigrew she'd been arguing with, Jolene would have to do some fast talking to keep him from spreading the news.

She was also aware if the same situation occurred late any other Sunday morning, she'd never have considered protecting Lyman. She'd have figured it was

Lady Guadalupe and the Sno-Kone Hut

his own, tough luck.

"Hello yourself, young lady." Mr. Atwater sat on the stool behind the register and didn't take his eyes from the newspaper in his hands.

"Jackson around anywhere?"

"Jackson?" Mr. Atwater peered over the top of his glasses. "Can't say as I've seen him." He folded the paper with a snap. "Thought I heard you speaking to someone."

"Oh, yeah." She shook her hands as if it was nothing. "It's just a friend of mine, got himself locked in his car at the Bacon last night and is still so sick, he couldn't go no farther." With effort, Jolene was able to lie. But never well, and to get anything past Granny she'd learned to stay as close to the truth as possible. She scanned the shelves on the back wall to buy time, got a pack of gum, unwrapped it and began to chew.

Mr. Atwater narrowed his eyes, looking stern. "Anything you need me to be doing about it?"

Jolene laughed. "No sir, he's harmless, I used to

date him. He's sleeping it off on the couch. I'd say let him be."

Still staring, he asked, "You sure there, Jolene? I could take him home with me when I leave."

"No, don't concern yourself none. I could beat him up with one hand tied behind me." The nervous laugh that followed didn't help.

Mr. Atwater shook his paper, disapproval dripping. "You sure?"

"Yes sir, I'm sure." Jolene thought maybe she should have come up with a story that didn't include intoxication, but then saw Jackson coming in.

Mr. Atwater looked up, nodded to Jackson and reopened his newspaper.

Jolene, delighted for the distraction, said too loudly, "Hey there Jackson, good to see ya."

Mr. Atwater stood up and waved Jackson over. "Listen here," he pushed his glasses to his bald head, "this young woman tells me some drunk is sleeping it off on her sofa, and I'd kindly appreciate it if you'd keep an eye on things after I leave out of here."

Mr. Atwater didn't look kind, he looked pissed off, and Jackson looked nervous. "Sure thing there, Mr. Atwater." Jackson shot eyes, wide and scared, at Jolene.

"Oh, my God, there's no looking after to be done." Jolene raised her arms and let them fall with disgust, then came from around the counter and signaled Jackson to follow. "We'd better get started. There's a lot to get done."

She shook her head after they got out of earshot. "I can't believe that man, he thinks he's my daddy."

"Or maybe granddaddy." Jackson chuckled.

Jolene and Jackson hitched a flatbed cart to the lawn tractor and began loading up tables from the storeroom. They'd been through the routine enough times to know what to do. After using so many different guys from the campground, Jolene was grateful for how well they worked together.

As the tractor pulled its load to the meadow, Jackson, driving, said, "Who's on your couch, anyone

I know?"

"Yeah, you probably do," Jolene said and didn't say more.

As they pulled around back, Jolene spotted Lyman's baby-blue car parked right up against her back porch. *He must have still been drunk when he parked.* "Oh, my God, stop, Jackson, stop."

Which Jackson promptly did, which made the cart slam into the tractor. "What's wrong?" he asked, then looked at where Jolene stared. "Oh. Whose is it?" Jackson asked, leaning over and speaking softly over the noise of the engine.

"Lyman Pettigrew, wait a minute." She jumped out and looked in the driver's side of the car. The keys were there. "Thank God," she muttered to no one at all, opened the door and got in, backing the car up to the woods where he usually parked, almost hidden. Then she pocketed the keys and came back to Jackson, hopping up on the tractor. "Thanks."

Jackson put the tractor back in gear. They trundled

Lady Guadalupe and the Sno-Kone Hut

over the rough path for a while before he asked, "Ain't that the guy that runs the bank?"

"Yeah, don't tell no one, will ya?"

"No, ma'am, I will not be telling anyone a thing." Jackson smiled, evidently unable to not enjoy his boss' discomfort.

"Especially not your father, or your mother."

"Especially not her, you're right about that, not a problem." Jackson continued to grin broadly.

Jolene couldn't remember him smiling that way before.

They unloaded the cart and began setting up tables, and stacking chairs. The trip was repeated four times before getting it done. The whole time, Jackson was more comfortable around her than she remembered, even to the point of looking her straight in the eye when he asked, "Daddy told me you were thinking about putting up a pavilion before too much longer?"

"Yeah, we've been talking about it. What do you think?"

"It'd be cheaper when you rent a tent."

"That's what your daddy said, and I agree."

"Might be a good bandstand, maybe get some people doing music. You might get a crowd on a Saturday night, good for a preacher on Sunday, too."

"I hadn't thought of that." Jolene looked up. "You're a lot like your daddy, you know?"

"Don't tell him that," Jackson snorted.

"No, I mean it. If he hadn't told me to get the campground going again, buy some trailers, I'd be out of business by now."

"I know, Miz Jolene."

Miz Jolene was the title they'd settled on. Jackson said calling her Jolene always pissed off his daddy and never felt right anyway. "Well, I appreciate a good idea, Jackson, thank you."

"You know, Miz Jolene," he wiped the sweat from his forehead. "I won't be telling your business to nobody, so don't you go worrying about it none."

"Thanks, Jackson."

Lady Guadalupe and the Sno-Kone Hut

"And while you're building that pavilion, how about putting a shed up next to them trees," he pointed to the line of tall evergreens on the property line, "big enough to hold all this stuff."

Jolene nodded her head, slowly. "Another good idea, the damned stockroom is getting crammed to the gills, and we wouldn't have to make these long trips."

"Yeah, it'd make it a lot easier on us working folk." Jackson smiled, including her in the comment.

Jolene smiled back, feeling better than she had since Lyman had fallen asleep. "Where'd you get that?" She touched the inside of his left forearm, where a tattoo of a cross with roses twining around it, resided.

"In prison."

"Who did it?"

"Me."

"You?"

"Yeah, I took my time with it. I was missing Momma some kind of bad and this, you know, felt like the closest thing to her. She always loved Jesus and her roses."

It didn't look like a crude tattoo she'd recognize coming from prison. In fact, it *did* look like Jackson's work, precise, patient and accurate. "You know I tried to kill you once."

"Yeah, Momma told me."

"She did?" Some part of Jolene wanting to be uniquely special to Miz Lorraine, and to have all her old secrets kept secret, didn't like hearing it at all.

But Jackson didn't notice. "Yeah, she said you set me out nekkid in the snow."

Jolene looked at the grass. "That's what I did," she admitted.

"Momma said you were some kinda jealous of me."

He still sounded happy. Jolene looked up at his handsome face. "It's true, I was," she said, "but I was only five."

"And I was only one."

Jolene smiled, realizing she'd been frightened of

Lady Guadalupe and the Sno-Kone Hut

Jackson. She hadn't recognized it before, but saw how his coming home after so many years locked up, unable to relax around anyone, much less with her, had made her wary. Yet, here was the Jackson he would have been if none of that had happened. Even if only for a moment, and it made her heart glad. Real glad.

Jackson was a big man, six-four at least, muscled, solid and the reason she'd hired him, they needed some muscle around the place. But for a while, she remembered the child she'd watched grow up.

"I was so jealous of you, I wanted you to disappear so I could have your momma all to myself again." She smiled at the truth of it. "You were supposed be some kinda doll baby I could play with, and you just disappointed me no end, Jackson, no end at all." She grinned.

"Well," Jackson's face still had the same handsome, peaceful smile. "I'm glad to be making up for it now."

They both turned when hearing a shout. "I got the

tent, where does it go?"

"Jackson, would you mind taking care of him?" Jolene asked.

"No ma'am, I would not."

"I think I'd better go tend to my guest."

"You do that, and I'll be seeing you tomorrow."

Jolene walked up the hill and went in the back door. Lyman was still passed out on the couch. She took the opportunity to take a shower, see if the new hair stuff worked away from Betty Lou's shop. She put on tan shorts with a lacy cream top Mrs. Olsen said would be fine for a casual supper.

*Casual was the word for it.* Jolene looked in the refrigerator and decided on French toast, bacon, and eggs. As quiet as she tried to be, Lyman woke up to bacon sizzling, French toast frying and syrup heating in a pan.

He groaned, stretching.

"How are you feeling?" Jolene asked, turning from the stove.

"Better, not bad at all, actually." Lyman stood

and stretched his hands over his head. He walked to the stove, leaning over Jolene's shoulder. "I hope you're making something for yourself. I'd hate to think you'd go hungry."

She smacked him with the spatula. "You're not funny. How about some OJ?"

"I'd like that."

"Go, sit at the table. I'll bring it to you."

Jolene filled a tall glass, set it by him and went back to the stove.

Lyman drained the glass. "Any coffee?"

"I'm making it." An enameled, light-blue coffee pot from nineteen forty-four sat next to the iron skillet with the French toast. She brought it to the table and placed it on a folded towel.

"Jolene, my God woman, you live in a previous century," Lyman said as she poured him a cup.

"What do you mean?" Jolene sat and poured her own.

"I guess I've never been around when you did

stuff."

"Are you still drunk?"

He shook his head, laughing. "No, no. I just never realized you used all these antiques in your everyday life."

"Antiques?"

"Even your coffee pot is an antique."

Jolene stared at the pot. It was chipped in spots, but not bad.

"Nobody makes coffee that way now. I have a machine at home and another one in my office that makes a cup of coffee for me with the touch of a button." He laughed, taking a sip.

"I've got the same kind of system out in that store there, buster, but it makes pots of coffee, and we don't need that much." She took a sip, frowning. "What's wrong, don't you like it?

"I like it fine. I just never understood you lived in another era. Seriously, I thought your place was charming, in a rough, rustic sort of way. I never realized it was *authentic*."

"What's that mean?" she asked darkly.

"It means what I'm saying, you live in another age."

"If you don't like it, then, don't drink it, Lyman."

"Oh, my, gosh, now don't go getting your feathers all ruffled. I'm not talking about the coffee." He took another sip. "I just didn't know how you lived before."

"Is there anything wrong with the way I live?"

"Not at all." He hesitated. "Except for stuff like a cell phone, which I *still* don't understand."

"I had one. I didn't like it."

"What in the world is there to dislike about convenience?"

Jolene shrugged, feeling her cheeks burn. "It messed me up, was all. I think some people aren't supposed to be around all that electricity." She set her cup down and went back to the stove, stabbing at the bacon with a fork. "Besides, I'm always here, and if for some reason I was able to get away, I sure don't want nobody calling me."

"Fine, not a problem, I get that. But how come you cook with your grandma's pots, live like your daddy, and his daddy did?"

"Cause nothing's broke. Dammit, Lyman, I'd get a new stove if this one stopped working."

"I know, I mean just for convenience sake, wouldn't you like an electric fry pan?"

"I wouldn't have nowhere to keep it." Jolene flipped the bacon over. It was nearly ready. She turned from the stove. "Listen here, Mr. Bank Manager, some of us out here don't get a regular paycheck, and when you're in business for yourself, you plow every nickel you got back into what feeds you."

She filled their plates. Lyman watched her expertly flip bacon, eggs and French toast on heavy white porcelain plates collected in nineteen thirty-three by an enterprising Great-grandmother from boxes of soap flakes. She'd sold the soap only after getting the pieces she wanted from each box and replacing them

## Lady Guadalupe and the Sno-Kone Hut

with pieces she didn't. Granny said there'd once been a twelve-piece place setting, with a triple set of serving piece. It had taken the rest of that Grandmother's life to use up all the soap.

Jolene's damp hair had curled into ringlets by the time she brought their plates to the table. Lyman was silent and didn't tear into his food like she expected. Before she could sit, he grabbed her hand and with a rough voice, like his throat was closing, said, "You look just like you did as a teenager, honey."

She felt oddly shy around a man who'd seen her naked more times than she could count.

"I'm sorry," he continued. "I didn't understand. I was being stupid, I guess, saying all that junk about cell phones and all."

"Don't worry about it." She grinned and sat. "But it's not my fault you've never been around here in the daylight before."

"You're right. It's all my fault."

"Speaking of daylight, I parked your car in the

woods." She pulled his keys from her pocket and put them next to his plate.

He stared at them. "Wow, I didn't even think about it."

"I know, weird huh?"

Soon Lyman was busy eating like a starving man, using French toast to sop up his eggs and then eating a second helping of French toast made properly with syrup and butter. He sat back, put his hand on his stomach and said, "I needed that, man did I need it."

Jolene smiled, finished her meal and heard gospel tunes starting up in the meadow.

Jolene and Lyman went to the back porch off her bedroom to better hear and were blessed to witness mist calmly rise from the river and meadow grass, in the cooler evening air. They sat on sun-warmed wooden steps, holding hands and watching purple clouds darken the horizon while listening to lovely sounds of five elderly men, in shiny maroon suits, singing, clapping, snapping their fingers and dancing to a rich rendition of,

Lady Guadalupe and the Sno-Kone Hut

*Coming Home to Jesus.*

The magic of good church was in the old tunes. That calming, restful peace descended on them, where worry vanished, and they were surely reminded the world was still a good place for humans to reside.

Chapter Seven

Daylight waned earlier. It was only a little after five, and already the sun was beginning to set. As if to clear it, Jolene shook her head. It *was*, after all, the fall Equinox, late September and the sun slanting exactly as it was supposed to that time of year. But somehow, even with the moon officially changing the seasons, no one had told the heat.

She longed to jump in the river with the boys, swinging from a shaggy rope tied to the old, leaning oak.

She'd only stepped outside for a moment, hoping it had cooled off, but nothing had diminished the damned heat, which went on and on relentlessly. Stagnant dirty air holding every speck of dust, exhaust and pollen from the entire summer. Mold and mildew spores clogging the

Lady Guadalupe and the Sno-Kone Hut

air, too, with mushrooms popping up everywhere.

An ancient, huge air conditioner built into the side wall of the Bait & Tackle, made so much racket she couldn't make out what the boys were shouting. As Jolene moved away from the air conditioner barely cooling the inside of the store, away from the heat blistering off a new blacktop parking lot, she saw Jackson pull up.

"You're here early." She smiled and waved.

Jackson got out of the Jeep, grabbing a rod and tackle box from the back. "Thought I'd get some fishing in first." He grinned and held up the tackle box. "Daddy even letting me borrow his stuff."

"Tell me, Jackson, do you see a grandmother down there?" Jolene pointed to the cove by the meadow.

"Too far away, can't tell."

"I'm gonna go check."

"I'll come with you. Daddy said the cattails over yonder was a good place to try for bass."

Walking down the hill beside Jackson, Jolene stared at the ground and smiled to herself. Jackson seemed to have taken hold of himself lately, and his daddy was acting like he might be noticing and might even be starting to forgive the son that broke his heart.

She'd caught Leon staring at Jackson, restocking the shelves. She'd seen the pain hidden far too long behind his eyes, finally visible.

Leon didn't know, and never would know about an infinitesimally tiny piece of red ribbon glued to the inside toe of his left work boot. Jolene put it there when the pump that watered the grounds stopped working, and he had waded barefoot under the fish house to fix it.

The ribbon was ancient, only fragments, really, of a silk Granny said possessed the power of regret. Granny made Jolene promise to use it wisely because it could create terrible repercussions. Jolene grinned, *so far, so good.*

Because of the unending heat, Jolene wore as little as she could get away with, shorts and a tank top, but even nakedness couldn't prevent the claustrophobia of heat pressing down. Just walking down a hill brought

## Lady Guadalupe and the Sno-Kone Hut

sweat dripping from her face. She wiped the sweat from her forehead with the back of her hand.

In addition to the weather, there was such a restlessness inside her she couldn't get shut off no matter what she did. Like wearing herself out helping Jackson and the Gutierrez boys finish up the boat slips, which even Leon was pleased with. Then taking a dose of Granny's tonic, which always worked, but hadn't. And then the unending hours of lying naked on the bed, fan blowing, with all that restlessness churning away, while trapped in a body too tired to move.

At some point, in the middle of the night, she'd called Lyman, hoping a good screw might calm down whatever had her all worked up. Old Lyman was eager to please. She had to give him that. She figured the invite must have gone to his head 'cause he came in and got to business with none of the usual awkwardness accompanying his visits.

She was surprised, was all, to have him knock on the back door, open her robe, wrap those warm hands of his around her naked body and begin kissing her before even stepping inside. Why, she was still a little dizzy from thinking about it. But then, she decided it was the heat and lack of sleep making her woozy.

Because even after Lyman left, kissing her gently at the back door and murmuring, "More than any man has loved any woman, I love you," sleep didn't come until sometime early that morning.

"There's a granny." Jackson pointed at a lady, so old the kids probably had to carry her in the chair she sat in.

Jolene shook her head, laughing. "Okay, I guess they got themselves an adult. I better get back." But a young boy at the very top of the oak, before it began its bend over the water, whooped and swung out. She was mesmerized. It was when he somehow clung to mid-air that fascinated her enough to forget about the unlocked store, the heat, her exhaustion, and Lyman.

Even the damned restlessness left as she watched the next boy time the exact moment to let go of that old

## Lady Guadalupe and the Sno-Kone Hut

rope and continue sailing up, like some sort of lovely bird. For one tiny nanosecond, he was suspended in mid-air, hands by his side, one leg pulled up, one pointing straight down. Jolene could see him clearly, hanging in the deep blue sky, then falling and crashing into the water, balled up like a bomb.

Jolene clapped. Jackson stuck his fingers in his mouth and blew a shrill whistle. She remembered her own child-self doing the exact same thing and figured Jackson was recalling the same. They stood side-by-side, watching boys like feral creatures, sure-footed, agile, climbing the ancient, enormous oak, reeling in the shaggy rope and leaping to oblivion.

All of them differing versions of the same dusky-skinned, black-headed child and all of them beautiful.

"Hey there, Mr. Jackson, Miz Gibson." A small boy yelled and waved from his spot on the tree. "Watch me."

Jolene waved back, thinking it was Mateo calling them.

"Watch me jump. I go the highest of anybody!" he hollered.

Jackson took a few steps forward. "Mateo! Be careful there, little dude."

"I no take chances. I'm the best there is." With a big whoop, Mateo jumped and stretched his tiny body across the sky in an arc. For Mateo there was no moment in the sky – he let go too soon, and was like an arrow going down, his feet pointing too straight, his arms too rigidly close to his sides.

Jolene stood twenty feet away and felt its wrongness. Jackson must have sensed it too, dropping his gear and taking slow steps towards the river. He craned his neck to see Mateo resurface. He stood on tiptoes and went closer to the water like a lion stalking prey. Nothing.

Jackson broke into a run and splashed in the water with his shoes on. Jolene could see him lose them as he fought his way through the shallows, then he dove and swam powerfully to where Mateo went down with

Lady Guadalupe and the Sno-Kone Hut

barely a splash. Jackson took a deep breath and dove under the water.

Jolene held her own breath, and then ran to the bank. The water's surface was undisturbed, and terror possessed her. She kicked off her flip-flops and waded out in the muck. She was the only one who moved. The boys ringed around her up the tree and on the grassy hill, were frozen, not speaking, barely breathing. The old woman in the chair was the same.

Jackson surfaced and took a series of quick, deep breaths, while treading water. His eyes met Jolene's, and a small shake of his head said everything.

"Oh, no," Jolene gasped involuntarily.

Jackson took a giant breath and dove forcefully into the dark river, but re-surfaced sooner than expected and was towing something. It was taking too long, so she waded out farther and when Jackson was close enough, grabbed his hand and pulled him towards the shallows. As soon as Jackson could get his feet under him, he brought Mateo's head up and out of the water. Jackson was exhausted and staggering in the muck.

Jolene took the boy in her arms. Two older boys ran down the bank and helped Jolene carry the lifeless body to the soft grass. Jackson climbed the bank on all fours and fell next to them, gasping for air, but Mateo wasn't breathing.

Jackson leaned over the boy, tilting his head and pinching his nose, covering the child's mouth with his own. Jackson's breath made a whooshing sound as Mateo's small chest rose.

Watching that skinny chest rise gave Jolene a powerfully grateful feeling. She grabbed the child's wrist. "He has a faint pulse."

Jackson nodded.

Jolene turned to one of the boys who'd come in the river, the tallest and skinniest one. "Run to the store and use the phone to call nine-one-one."

The boy stared, growing pale.

"Do this," she shouted. "Go to the phone on the counter and push nine-one-one. It'll be okay. Let them

Lady Guadalupe and the Sno-Kone Hut know we had a drowning. Go!"

The boy nodded and turned.

"Run," she yelled, and he did. Jolene looked back to Mateo and watched Jackson trying to breathe the life back into him. She felt Mateo's pulse growing weaker, and fear filled her a second time. "We're running out of time."

Something gathered in Jolene, an urge to get the river out of the child so she wouldn't be able to call him away, built in her. She became certain if they didn't, Mateo was doomed.

"Let me take a turn Jackson, give you a rest."

Jackson straightened and took a breath for himself. "Good idea."

Jolene stood, snatching Mateo by his heels, fast, before Jackson could ask why, or stop her. She stood and held Mateo upside down.

"Hit his back," she screamed. "Harder," she yelled over the screeches of the old granny, who'd come to her senses.

Jackson did, Mateo coughed, and water streamed from his mouth. Jolene set him on the grass, his head to the bank, downhill. He coughed again then threw up a gallon of river. Mateo began crying. So did Jolene, hugging the boy to her, unbearably grateful to him for being alive.

Mateo pushed Jolene away. The child looked deeply into her eyes.

Jolene's heart broke, so quick and unexpected, it was shocking. Like the river gushing from the child, her heart released pain. She cried out, one, long howl. Mateo screamed his anguish, while Jolene remembered their losses.

How Daddy left so quick, and that boy who went to the Army and never came home, Jackson to prison, Lorraine and Leon to their own private hell, Granny gone, after losing pieces of her for so damned long, old Mrs. Gunther and nearly everyone she'd ever been close to, gone.

In Mateo's scream was loss of his old life; his

Lady Guadalupe and the Sno-Kone Hut

village, his *la abuela*, cousins and friends. But, even though his eyes were filled with tears, they were also reassuring.

Some part of Jolene wondered at a six-year-old, reassuring a grown woman after what they'd both just been through, and *he was the one who drowned.*

Jackson squatted next to them, a look of bewilderment and relief on his face. "You okay there?" he asked both of them.

"I saw her." Mateo's voice was raspy.

In Jolene's mind, a glorious vision appeared: Mary, the Mother of Jesus, in blue and gold billowing robes with a bright light extending all around her smiling, loving presence.

"Lady Guadalupe," Mateo said plainly, still staring in Jolene's eyes and ignoring the old woman babbling in Spanish, trying to take him. "You see her too."

"Yes, in your eyes, I see her." The vision did not recede. Jolene saw the face of a young boy and saw the Holy Mother, too, in an almost a super-imposed manner around the child. She was a powerful presence, comforting in some lovely, timeless manner, with a sense of peace almost frightening in its depth. "Such love," Jolene said. Mateo nodded and smiled.

She grabbed his face and kissed him. She laughed and kissed him again, on his cheeks, his forehead, his ears, and cried tears feeling so good to cry, she never wanted to stop.

Jackson put his hand on Jolene's shoulder. "I'll go up and meet the ambulance."

Jolene didn't want to break the contact with Mateo and hesitated before turning to Jackson, smiling. "Good idea."

"You okay?" he asked.

"Never better, I swear."

"The lady, she was there," Mateo said again in his raspy voice and pointed at the water.

"I know." And she did.

"She was, she was so beautiful." The little boy

Lady Guadalupe and the Sno-Kone Hut dissolved into tears, everything finally being too much for his few years.

Jolene hugged Mateo, who was beginning to tremble and was probably going into shock. To three of the bigger boys, she said, "Go up to the store and go in the back. Get blankets from the chest at the foot of my bed and bring them here."

They turned and ran like a highly drilled military unit.

The ambulance arrived, and the crew carried a gurney down the hill. Jolene couldn't have said how long she'd been holding Mateo or smiling into his eyes. She loved the child, pure and simple. The old lady couldn't separate them. Mateo waved off the other boys, saying, "Vamoose." It was lovely until Mateo was pulled from her and promptly began howling again. The emergency crew put him on a gurney and Mateo continued yelling until Jolene was able to get hold of his hand. She held it all the way to the parking lot. Mateo screamed again when she had to let go so they could put him in the ambulance. Charlie Moses, the driver, allowed Jolene to ride in the back to the hospital, hoping Mateo might quiet down again.

They put an oxygen mask over his mouth and nose, but his large, brown eyes continued to stare into Jolene's, even after they got him to the hospital. And she continued to look into his, and hold his hand, smiling the entire time. She knew he wasn't scared. He needed her. She needed him as well. The connection between them was that powerful, that comforting.

It wasn't until his mother was found and brought to her son's room that the connection between her and Mateo broke. The moment his mama bent over the bed, dripping tears and gathering the child to her, it was gone.

Jolene was surprised it ended so quickly, as relatives poured around Mateo and nudged her away. The people streaming into the room didn't notice as Jolene slipped away.

Leaving the hospital, the darkness outside startled her too. She wondered how late it was and stood in front

Lady Guadalupe and the Sno-Kone Hut

of the hospital, thinking on who she should call for a ride when Jackson pulled up in her daddy's truck.

"I got an Aunt working at the hospital to call me when you left," he said, pushing open the passenger door. "She called, and here I am."

"Thanks, Jackson." Jolene got in the truck, feeling strange sitting on that side and wishing she knew what Jackson thought about the day's events. She knew the day had left her feeling as jumbled as she'd ever been in her life.

"How you doing, Miz Jolene?"

"Quit calling me that. Screw your dad. My name's Jolene." She hadn't expected to say it but acted like she meant every word.

Jackson laughed, but nervously, as he put the truck in gear. "Well, I'm glad to see you ain't lost none of your feistiness."

Jolene shrugged, unsure where all her vehemence was coming from. "It's my name, you always called me Jolene, or at least that is," she turned, grinning and wondering where this new personality was coming from, "since you could say it right."

"I know. Momma told me I called you Jo-meanie, or something. Quit picking on me, I was just a little kid."

"Jo-weenie is what you called me."

His smile, when a car passed them, and their lights illuminated his face, was Jolene's first miracle. All her little-brother feelings for Jackson were restored, full-blown, intact. He went from being a man who worked for her, to *Jackson*, the little boy who'd follow her anywhere, up any creek, through any woods, with an unwavering belief in her ability to bring them home safely, which she always did.

And she knew where to lead him again. "Jackson?"

"Yeah?"

Another car passed, Jolene noticed the bags under his eyes and saw an exhaustion she fully understood. "You know your daddy and mine, were what they called 'rounders' back when they was young."

Lady Guadalupe and the Sno-Kone Hut

Jackson gave Jolene an appraising glance. "Yeah, but mine cleaned up his act and yours."

"Mine didn't," she interrupted, "he died from it. Might as well say it. It's the truth and it don't hurt none anymore."

"I was there, It surely did at the time."

"I know." Jolene stared in her lap. "I mean it don't hurt no more to talk about."

"Well that's a good thing, Jolene. I'm glad to hear it 'cause I worried about you after. . . everything happened."

"You sticking around would have helped, I know. Losing Daddy, then you and your parents, too, Jackson. It was like I lost them for a while after you got locked up. It felt, I don't know, *unfair* at times." She looked out the window, remembering those days. "Your momma scared to death for you, your daddy hardly speaking to no one, Daddy dead and Granny ailing." She looked at him. "Sometimes Jackson, sometimes it felt like just a little too much for all of us."

"I know, and it was the worst part of the whole deal."

"I guess what I'm trying to say is, we all paid. Not just you, but me, your parents, all of us."

Jackson sighed. "Sometimes the burden of it just…"

"That's my point Jackson. You got to put down that burden. You know what happened, your daddy weren't a whole lot better than mine for most of your childhood, and then he gets so damned high and mighty, it might have been him that drove Daddy to his last binge. And maybe he drove you to do what you did too."

Jackson stared out the windshield.

"You got to put it down, find some way to. You saved a child's life today." He started to interrupt, but Jolene shook her head and waved her arms to get him to shut up. "No, damn it, you found him down there. I don't know how, but you did."

"The second time I went down, it was like he was put in my arms." Jackson's voice went soft, lost its timber. "The first time, I had a real bad feeling, like I

## Lady Guadalupe and the Sno-Kone Hut

knew he was dead. It's the worst feeling in the world, don't I know it." Jackson shook his head. "But then, there he was in my arms like some sort of gift."

"Did you feel her Jackson?"

"Her?"

"Mateo met the Holy Mother Mary, he called her Lady Guadalupe, down there."

Jackson took a deep breath and let it out. "I felt something, Lord, yes. Something real kind." He looked at Jolene and smiled. "And with a Momma like mine, that's saying something." Jackson stared out the open window into the dark night. "That kindness was deeper than anything I'd ever known, its gentleness startled me some, I have to admit, but then I had to get that boy out of there."

"Yeah," Jolene nodded, smiling. "You had to save his life, which you did." She hesitated, then heard her own voice take on a gentleness she'd not known. "And now it's time to forgive yourself, Jackson, and forgive us, me, your parents, anyone hurt by the loss of you. You got to forgive us for our hurting. You got to forgive yourself too, for being a hurt kid and for making mistakes."

Jackson raised his chin, narrowing his eyes with concentration and staring at the road ahead.

She went on, more confident in the message she was delivering. "I don't think being involved with Lady Guadalupe, or whoever she is, was an accident for either of us."

"I've been wondering about that since the ambulance left."

"Wondering what?"

"The whole thing felt… pre-arranged or something."

"Pre-arranged. Yeah, it did." The enormity of the day hit her as she spoke and she grabbed Jackson's hand to ground herself and not fly away with it all.

Jackson looked at her, alert. "Hey, now, there, Jolene, what's going on? You okay?"

After a few deep breaths, she nodded. "Yeah, I'm okay. Everything today was just a lot, you know?"

Lady Guadalupe and the Sno-Kone Hut

"Don't I though."

She took another deep breath and grabbed his hand tighter. "I'm sitting here next to you and find myself compelled, Jackson, I mean, you *have* to hear this, it was a sign. You have to forgive everyone, including yourself. This ain't crazy talk, it's just the plain truth."

Jackson squeezed her hand. "I think you're right about that." He smiled. "Down there in the dark with that boy in my arms, I never felt better. That boy and me were surrounded in pure sweet love and nothing else."

"That place, Jackson? Who you were right then? That's you."

Jackson held Jolene's hand differently, like he had as a child, trusting.

"You're right. I need to let it go, all of it." He smiled broadly, took in another deep breath and let it out. "All the crap I put you-all through, all the crap I went through, all the losses *I* made for others, the wasted time, gone forever… it's got to be over with sometime, and I guess now's as good as any."

Jolene smiled.

"But what was the message for you in all that stuff?"

Which was something she'd been studying on all day. "I don't rightly know for sure yet. All I know is I feel dizzy from spirit right now."

"I imagine you do. Yes, ma'am, I imagine you do."

Jackson let go of her hand so he could downshift as they turned onto the dirt road leading to the Bait & Tackle.

Jolene felt gritty from the sweat and dirt still clinging to her. She was glad she'd be home soon. "I've been thinking on this a while now and come Spring, when they start fishing again, how about coming in full-time, start taking the load off your daddy?"

Jackson grinned and shook his head. "That sounds mighty nice, Jolene." He laughed. "This has been some kinda day, and that's all I can say. I'm glad we don't have too many of these, because I swear, I don't think I could take it. Feels like the whole world got turned upside down or something."

"I agree."

After Jackson pulled up to where Jolene parked next to the store, they both got out. Jackson locked the door and tossed the keys to Jolene. He looked as relaxed and happy as he'd been as a child. "We had us some kind of *experience*, ain't we?"

She met his eyes over the truck's hood. "Yes, we have. Take tomorrow off Jackson, with pay. You deserve it."

"That sounds real good, but you never answered my question."

"What's that?"

"How you doing, there, Jolene?"

She stood in her muddied clothes and thought. "I'm fine Jackson, and as long as I got people like you and your family around to count on, I'm gonna continue on being just fine."

"All right, then, sounds good to me."

Jolene used her key to unlock the store, waved to Jackson as he drove away in his daddy's Jeep, then locked the store again.

The river was calling her, as it sometimes did. She always answered. Down the path past the fish house, to the beach, she went. The entire way, croaking frogs sang in the same manner as always, the soft, humid air felt like the same blanket of warmth it had been for a while, and the quiet river still flowed. She understood there was nothing malevolent in the water. There never had been. When a river took and what a river gave back, were both parts of being a living water.

In her mind's eye, she saw Mateo's brown ones, radiant with spirit, his face lit with joy. He hadn't been the tiniest bit afraid. The Lady had been too much for a small child, but only a child that young could have seen her. She'd understood this the first moment of looking in his eyes.

Mateo knew he'd been brought back to share his vision. It had been her job and Jackson's, to bring him

## Lady Guadalupe and the Sno-Kone Hut

back. Jolene sighed. There was some plan unfolding she couldn't begin to guess at, but she already knew her part was to go along, no matter what. And like Mateo, she didn't have to be afraid.

She waded out to where the water came up to her knees, and the sand stopped, planning to wash away the day's mud and sweat, before taking a shower. Instead, she sat in the water, fully dressed and felt her legs relax. She put her hands behind her, to lean back and look at the stars and her left hand felt something. She picked it up.

It was some sort of child's toy – a plastic figure a couple of inches tall, which she slipped in her wet pocket. It was too dark to see what it was. The stars overhead in the black night winked as she floated, remembering the day and feeling so peaceful she worried about falling asleep right there in the water.

Jolene stripped on the screened-in porch and dropped her clothes on the cement floor. It wasn't until the following morning when sorting clothes for the wash, Jolene found the figurine in her pocket – a tiny statue of

Lady Guadalupe. A small child with upraised arms was at her feet. He looked like Mateo.

The statue had seen better days, some of her paint was gone. "Thank you," she said to the spirits as Granny had taught her. Granny said she'd see days of wonder in her lifetime. Jolene wished she understood how Granny had known.

Jolene wasn't sure how long she stood next to the cupboard Daddy built off the porch for the washer and dryer, staring at a small figurine. She came back to herself when the bell over the front door rang out in the empty store. Hurriedly, she put Lady Guadalupe in the pocket of the shorts she had on. The rest of the day, every time she felt wobbly, she'd wrap her fingers around the figurine in her pocket, until she felt whole again.

It was a comfort, was all, just a real comfort.

## Chapter Eight

Beginning on Monday, the Bait & Tackle was cleaned out of groceries by the end of each day, and every day the meadow held more and more people. Jolene hired two of Jackson's cousins to help out at the store, while Leon and Jackson called on other relatives to help with the meadow.

Mateo's vision spread like wildfire among the Hispanic community; pilgrims came to view where Lady Guadalupe had appeared.

Cars and trucks jammed the parking lot and road. Leon opened the pasture above the meadow for additional parking; it was knee deep in grass with no time to mow. Yet soon, it too filled with vehicles of every make and model, and still they kept coming, crammed with every age of person, from frail infants to the frail elderly.

Jolene had been putting in sixteen and seventeen hour days, and it wasn't enough to keep up with the flood.

"Jolene?"

Jolene wondered what horrible news Jackson had for her this time. "Yeah?" She signaled Rosalee to take over the register and took a few steps away.

"The porta-potty guys just called. They can't get their truck through. The damned road is too jammed with parked cars. I hooked up the sludger and emptied a few of the porta-potties, but I can't keep ahead of them filling up again. Our people are letting them use their trailers, but you know," Jackson sounded scared, "that won't be holding up much longer."

He had every reason to be frightened as they were headed for a sewage nightmare. "What's the mood out there?"

"Oh," Jackson took a deep breath and dropped

# Lady Guadalupe and the Sno-Kone Hut

his shoulders. "I'd say it's going all right, everything considering. The weather couldn't be better, and at least there's that. I can't make out what anyone is saying, of course, but they are a calm bunch, no shouting or nothing like any of my folks do in church." He smiled. "They got themselves a Catholic Priest down there, did you know?"

"I only hope they got a few doctors down there too. What're we gonna do if someone needs medical help? No ambulance could get through now."

Jackson shook his head. "Don't be borrowing trouble. We got enough to deal with as it is."

"They only paid to park, the ones on the road didn't even do that. You think I'll be liable if something happens?"

Jackson put his hands on her shoulders. "Jolene, you gotta stop. We can't do nothing about it, so let's deal with what we can, all right?"

*How in the hell do we deal with this?* Jolene stuck her hand in her pocket, searching for and finding

Lady Guadalupe. She took a deep breath. "You're right." Jackson sounded so much like his father, she could relax a little. "What's your biggest problem right now?"

"Where to put the shit?" He grinned.

"That's a good question."

"I've filled up those big coolers from the fish house and man I hated doing it." He shook his head again. "I only used them 'cause they got lids, and trust me, we need lids. Now I don't know what else to put it in."

Jolene pondered on the question. "How about dragging the horse trough over in the woods and filling it?"

"People are already over there and they kinda leaking next door too."

"Then I don't know." She looked up at him. "I guess that's why I haven't seen a delivery truck all day, they can't get though, either."

"Well, yeah."

Lady Guadalupe and the Sno-Kone Hut

"Sorry, it takes a while for my brain to catch up with me these days." She turned and saw nothing to keep cold behind the glass doors, a few canned goods remained on the shelves, but only the section with fishing poles and tackle looked as it had a week ago. A few packs of cigarettes were left on the wall behind her and some odd pieces of candy, but the safe in the floor of Daddy's room was stuffed with cash.

"Let's close it down. There ain't nothing left to sell anyway. We'll close the store and announce it's over, tell everyone to go home."

"I don't know as they'd listen."

Which was, they knew, the real problem. Jolene and Jackson, went out front to study on the matter.

"When it gets dark, we could cut off the lights, maybe that would work," Jackson said. "But then again, maybe they wouldn't even care if it was dark."

"Let's go talk to your daddy. The residents are used to listening to him. Maybe he can get them to get the others moving out." Jolene stuck her head in the door. "Rosalee? Lock up when you're done with your customer and bring me the keys, will you?"

Rosalee nodded.

Jolene and Jackson went around the store. The sight of the throngs hugging the hillside took Jolene's breath away. "Oh, my God."

"Told you."

"It's even worse today, a lot worse."

They wove cautiously through the crowd, searching for Leon.

Jolene sensed gentleness among them. Most faced the river where Lady Guadalupe appeared to Mateo, yet they weren't like zombies or acting oddly. They spoke softly to each other, keeping an eye on children playing in the margins of blankets spread on the ground. As they made their way through the meadow, the occupants of lawn chairs or people stretched out on blankets, tried to get out of the way as much as possible, smiling.

It took a while, but eventually they found Leon

Lady Guadalupe and the Sno-Kone Hut in the fish house, behind a locked door.

"Sorry," he said, unlocking it. "I needed a break."

"Don't worry, I understand," Jolene said.

Both the fish house and the fishing pier extending behind it, were built on stilts to accommodate high waters when they came. People were two and three deep around the pier's railings. Children ran, playing games of tag in the middle. Jolene worried the whole thing might collapse from the sheer weight of all the folks up there and explained her plan to get them gone.

"They ain't gonna listen to me, Jolene," Leon said, rubbing his bald head and replacing his cap. "They ain't gonna care if it's dark. They don't care about nothing but seeing that Guadalupe thing. They ain't even got much left to eat, but I don't see that changing a damn thing. I got buckets of water circulating for them to drink. And, I'm worried something awful about a few of the old ones out there." He threw up his hands. "But nobody else is, and I'm plumb out of ideas."

"But what about the residents? You could get with them – explain it isn't healthy for all these people to stay, we're out of options, stuff like that?"

A roar from the crowd pulled them to a side door of the fish house, where a small, tacked on porch overlooked the river. The throngs were standing, children and babies in arms. Other arms extended to pull up the elderly. Everyone's attention was on the lake. A loud babble of excited Spanish spiked, then went silent, as a large shadowy shape filled the air above the river.

To Jolene and the people perched with her above the river, it looked like a mist as it lifted. A cool, green, refreshing mist.

The shape drifted higher and like an odd-colored cloud in the breeze floated upriver. The excited throngs milled as if deciding how to follow.

"Did you see that?" Jolene yelled over the noise, as animated as everyone in the meadow.

"Lord, yes." Jackson and Leon, said in unison,

Lady Guadalupe and the Sno-Kone Hut then looked at each other in surprise, brows raised.

"I think she's leaving." Jolene felt wonderfully happy.

The three leaned on the porch railing and watched the crowd mass like starlings and begin flowing uphill to the pasture and up the rough trail to the store, away from the meadow.

"I think we should close up for a few days," Jolene said.

"Good idea." Jackson and his father said in unison again, this time not looking at each other.

"I'm gonna call the septic tank guy to come out tomorrow. Jackson, can you take care of him, let the residents know what's going on?"

"Be here tomorrow? Sure thing."

"You and me?" Jolene turned to Leon, touching his arm. "We're going to take a few days off."

Leon started to object, but Jolene cut him off. "I don't want to hear no more about it. I'm worn down to a nub, and you are too. Lorraine has been alone all week, and you need to go home."

Leon sighed, shook his head. "You're right. I'm tuckered out."

"It's okay, old man." Jolene giggled, enjoying her joy.

They went inside the fish house. "I don't know how long it will take to clean things up around here. Jackson?" she asked. "How long do you think we should close up? Maybe cancel the reunion on Sunday?"

"I don't rightly know, yet."

"Well, whatever, you decide. You're the one in charge the next few days. Hire as many people as you need. I'll call the distributor tomorrow and tell them to expect to get their orders from you for a while." Jolene sighed, remembering the mist lifting from the river and the freedom she tasted. "I gotta get out of here."

"You'd better sit tight there, girl. It'll take a while for the traffic to clear out," said Leon.

"I know. I'll take a shower and wait a bit. I'd

Lady Guadalupe and the Sno-Kone Hut offer you-all something to eat, but there's nothing left."

Leon shook his head. "Don't worry about it." He clapped Jackson on the arm. "I think that loser cousin of yours, Antione, is parked out on River Road. How about we try catching a ride with him?"

"Good idea, Daddy."

Leon locked the doors to the fish house. and they went up the ramp, joining people streaming up the path. They separated at the top, and Jolene found Rosalee sitting on the cement steps to the screened-in porch. "Sorry, ma'am, I couldn't get down there, too many people coming up."

"That's okay. Come on inside, you might as well be comfortable. Where's your sister?"

"She's trying to catch a ride. I was waiting for you." She handed Jolene the keys.

They went through the porch and Jolene unlocked the door to her kitchen. "Tell her and everyone else who helped out, to keep their time until they get home and give their hours to Jackson. I'll get everyone a check the day after tomorrow, okay?"

Rosalee smiled as she followed Jolene inside. She had a pretty smile, all the Bookers did. "That'd be fine ma'am."

"Would you like some tea or something?"

"Yes, ma'am, that would be nice. I came in with Jackson, so I guess we're all stuck here for a while."

"Um, Jackson and Leon are looking for someone, Antione, I think they said, for a ride home."

"Then, I better be seeing if I can't catch up with them. Thanks anyway, Miz Gibson." Rosalee smiled again and quickly went through the curtains, the store and out the front door.

Jolene followed, with her keys still in her hand, only intending to lock up behind Jackson's cousin. But instead, she went out front with Rosalee. "Thanks again for all your help."

"Glad for the work, thank *you*, ma'am." She waved, before disappearing down the drive at a quick pace.

Lady Guadalupe and the Sno-Kone Hut

The crowd in the parking lot had thinned, more elderly mixed in, walking slower and holding onto someone's arm. Sleeping babies and children were carried in the arms of mothers, fathers and older siblings. Jolene sensed the same joy in her, in each of them. Instead of going back inside she locked the store, pocketing the keys with her Lady Guadalupe and walked with them down the driveway to the road. She hadn't planned on following them for any length of time, she was only unwilling to leave the current of peace she found herself in.

The popping noise of motorcycles and motorbikes were the only sounds and forms of transportation able to weave through the cars double parked on both sides of the street.

Jolene shook her head, amazed. She wandered another half-mile before she saw vehicles moving and never spotted Leon, Jackson or Rosalee again. She recognized one face, Mr. Gutierrez, sitting by himself in his pickup. Jolene came up to his window. "Hey there,

Mr. Gutierrez."

He was startled, his eyes widening. "Miz Gibson, I did not expect to see you."

"Are you trying to get home?"

"*Si*, I had to work this morning."

Jolene looked around at the congestion. "I think it's gonna be a while."

Mr. Gutierrez sighed. "*Si*, you are right."

"I'd pay you to turn around, take me into town."

Mr. Gutierrez looked surprised. "*Si*, I would be glad to."

"Thanks." Jolene smiled and got in the ancient pick-up.

It took some grinding of gears, but Mr. Gutierrez was able to turn the truck around. "What happened?" he asked, nodding at the stream of traffic heading away from the campground.

"She left."

"Lady Guadalupe?"

"Yes, she came up from the water like a green

Lady Guadalupe and the Sno-Kone Hut cloud and went up the river."

"You saw this?"

"Yes, it was very, very cool."

Mr. Gutierrez shook his head. "I should have stayed, Maria said so, but I didn't listen."

"I think everyone is trying to figure out where she went."

"So maybe I'll have a second chance?"

"Maybe, I don't know."

"Are you searching for her?"

"No, I'm just tired of the place and hungry. By the way, the Bait & Tackle is out of food and won't open again for a few days. Will you let everyone know?"

"Certainly. Where would like me to take you?"

"Drop me off at the Woolworth's, please. I'll get something there."

"Not a problem." Mr. Gutierrez' truck rattled through town and pulled up in front of the old brick building.

Jolene got out, went around to the driver's side while pulling a wad of large bills from her pocket. She handed Mr. Gutierrez a fifty through his open window. "Thanks, I appreciate it."

He took it, looked at the bill and with worried eyes said, "This is too much."

Jolene laughed. "It's the smallest bill I got on me. Take it, I appreciate the ride."

"How will you get home? I could come back if you'd like."

She smiled. "Thanks, but I think I'll call Mr. Booker's house," which was what the residents called Leon, "and get Jackson, or someone, to drive me home."

He held up the fifty. "Gracias for this, Miz Gibson, call if I can help in any way."

She grinned. "How about lending me five bucks for dinner?"

Mr. Garcia grinned back and pulled his wallet from his back pocket. Retrieving a five dollar bill, he

Lady Guadalupe and the Sno-Kone Hut held it to her. "Will this be enough?"

"Thanks. It'll be plenty."

The grinding of unmeshed gears accompanied the truck's departure.

Jolene went inside.

"Hey there, Jolene."

Patsy Cord had run the restaurant since Jolene was in school.

"Hey there, Miz Cord." It was four in the afternoon, and the place was deserted except for an elderly gentleman Jolene knew, but couldn't place.

Patsy pushed off the back counter and came where Jolene sat, wiping the clean counter with a dry cloth. "I saw on the news where there was a bunch of commotion out at your place."

"You can say that again."

"And that you and Jackson Booker, saved some little Mexican boy from drowning."

"Yep." Jolene felt shy. "But Jackson did most of it."

"Sounds like a busy week. What can I get you?"

The cheeseburger, fries and cold coke were delicious. Patsy didn't ask a lot of questions, for which Jolene was also grateful.

"What kind of pie do you have?" Jolene asked.

"Coconut and one slice of banana cream."

"I'll take the banana cream."

"You got it."

Jolene finished her pie, and not ready to go home, wandered the building. She ended up at the thrift store, which had real doors, unlike the curtains and alcoves scattered around.

Pulling a door open, she noticed Connie Plunkett and Evelyn Cobb behind the register's counter.

They didn't even attempt not to look like they were staring at Jolene's wrinkled shorts and T-shirt, and she sensed superiority rising from the area and suspected it would be only moments before disapproval rained down on her.

Evelyn Cobb's wavering, old-lady voice said,

Lady Guadalupe and the Sno-Kone Hut

"Howdy-doo, Jolene."

Jolene stuck her hand in her pocket, wrapped her fingers around Lady Guadalupe and felt reassured. "Hey there, Mrs. Cobb," she said loudly and nodded. *She's only a harmless old lady. I needn't lump her in with the likes of Connie, who's an actual, real bitch.* "How're you doing Mrs. Cobb? I haven't seen you in a while."

Mrs. Cobb, who had always been heavy-set, was now completely fat, her flowered cotton dress straining mightily at the seams. "I'm doing tolerable, Jolene. I've got the arthritis something awful, though."

"Sorry to hear it. I miss seeing you and Mr. Cobb." They used to come to the Bait & Tackle occasionally and rent a boat for fishing.

"I miss those days, and him, too, honey. Thanks for remembering."

"Can I help you find something, Jolene?" Connie's voice was shrill, as always.

"I really don't think you can," Jolene

said back. "Thanks anyway." She went to the racks where Mrs. Olsen had taken her, glad they were on the other side of the building. She selected items that appealed simply because she liked the fabric. Jolene hardly noticed she was drawn to soft pastels and flowery prints.

She took the items to the dressing room and tried on a skirt made of some sort of filmy yellow fabric with small blue and white flowers. She liked it and twisted in front of the mirror admiring how she looked. A white eyelet peasant blouse went nicely on top. Even her yellow flip-flops looked better with what she had on.

Jolene spent every day of her life in shorts, or jeans. A skirt, swishing around her ankles felt different, sort of liberating.

She kept three skirts, all with tiny, wrinkled pleats, and found tops that went with them. Jolene considered changing back into her shorts, but put the yellow skirt and eyelet top, back on instead.

Lady Guadalupe and the Sno-Kone Hut

"Jolene, what in the world are you wearing?"

"Clothes, Connie." Jolene said sternly, as she slapped the tags she'd ripped off her outfit and the other clothes on the counter. She held her shorts and T-shirt under her arm. In her hand was Lady Guadalupe and the wad of money.

"You're not supposed to wear our stuff out of here."

"I don't see no sign saying I can't."

Connie frowned. "I've just never seen anyone wear something without paying for it first. She began ringing up the sale.

"I'm standing here, trying to pay you. I'm not planning on walking out with anything I don't buy."

"There *should* be some sort of rule against it. I don't think that's even sanitary. I'd never wear someone else's clothes. Not without washing them first. Why, you don't even know who they used to belong to."

For just a moment, for only long enough to see

it, Jolene felt the kick in her stomach. For only a little bit longer, she felt the wrongness Connie and her ilk had placed on her shoulders.

She pulled the hand with Lady Guadalupe and the wad of cash to her heart and saw it all differently. Different in an odd sort of way, but immediately different. Connie was still the person who'd delighted in tormenting her, only she was transparent. Jolene couldn't look at her without seeing a woman who feared so much, it made her hate. Saw it plain as day. The way Connie held herself so rigidly, she was nearly spastic. Tension bristled from her, in waves of the misery she refused to acknowledge.

Jolene said, "Thanks for being so concerned and all about my sanitation there, Connie."

Connie gave her a sharp-eyed glance as Evelyn toddled back from the other end of the counter, where she'd been fussing with some jewelry.

"You look real nice there, Jolene," Mrs. Cobb said.

Lady Guadalupe and the Sno-Kone Hut

"Thanks, Mrs. Cobb." Jolene's eyes darted to the older lady, and she gave her a brief nod.

"I thought that was a real good thing you and that colored man of yours did, saving that boy." Mrs. Cobb had her hands clasped in front of her like a child. A very large, very round child.

Jolene's spine stiffened. "Jackson Booker was the one who fetched him from the water, breathed the life back into him. I only helped," she said clearly.

Mrs. Cobb's eyes grew large. "In the newspaper, Jackson said it was you who done it."

"Don't believe everything you read, Mrs. Cobb, he was only being humble and giving credit where it wasn't due."

"Oh." Evelyn Cobb shut up.

"That," Connie said in a flat voice, "will be seventeen-fifty."

"Take it from the hundred," Jolene said, placing a bill on the table.

"I don't think we can make change for that

much." Connie's face reddened. She was nearly screaming, "This is a *charity*, Jolene. We can't change a hundred dollar bill."

Jolene gripped Lady Guadalupe tighter. "Well, I know I'm just as sorry as I can be about that." Jolene marveled at how little *it did* matter to her. She felt light and free and nearly laughed when saying, "How 'bout I donate the whole bill to this here *charity* and we'll call it a day?"

"We've got those two fifties in the back," Evelyn offered.

Connie turned on the woman, glaring.

Jolene noticed Connie's hair needed to go to her beauty parlor, a lot of grey outlined her face and even the colored parts were greasy-looking.

Connie never hesitated to spend a nickel on herself. Jolene hadn't even known it *was* a dye job, because, somehow, Connie's beautician managed to keep the same highlights of red in it. So why was she suddenly letting herself go?

Lady Guadalupe and the Sno-Kone Hut

"What the hell, Evelyn?" Connie barked.

But Evelyn Cobb didn't appear to catch her meaning. "I'll get us one," she said, lifting up the hinged part of the counter.

Jolene assisted, as Evelyn's bulk prevented Connie from reaching around and helping, or hindering her efforts. Evelyn grunted softly as she shoved herself through the opening. "Be right back," she said a little breathlessly.

"You know, there's been some talk in my women's prayer group about you." Connie leaned on the counter, looking at her immaculate fingernails, picking at a non-existent cuticle.

"How exciting for you," Jolene said, and felt rather pleased at her quick response. She stuffed her shorts and T-shirt in the bag with her other clothes.

Connie looked up from her nails. "Well, not exactly about you, but about those Mexicans you keep at your place."

"What about them?"

"Crime, Jolene, crime is what. You have no business bringing them so near our town. There was some talk about shutting you down."

Jolene's campground followed every rule and regulation. Leon made sure of it, so there was little chance of that happening. She figured Connie was only trying to shake her up and wondered why.

"And the kids. Our schools aren't set up for immigrants. Why should our tax dollars go to helping a bunch of foreigners who can't even speak English?"

"Those people pay taxes, too. So does my campground and store."

"You know what I'm saying. It's a nuisance. They all are."

Jolene stared at her old nemesis and felt only sadness. "I bet you didn't know I could tell when a Latino family got to America." Jolene marveled at the calmness in her voice. And the pity she had for the miserable woman in front of her.

"Oh, please, I know you consider yourself some

## Lady Guadalupe and the Sno-Kone Hut

kind of psychic, Jolene, but that's just ridiculous."

"Nothing psychic about it. All I have to do is see how tall their kids are and I can tell."

"What kind of mumbo-jumbo are you talking about now?"

"If the kids are tall they've been here a while."

"Who cares?"

"Their parents do. Parents are real proud of their tall kids, 'cause it means they got fed."

"Jolene, you're making this up."

"No, I'm not. Lots of times the older ones are short like their parents, but you can see younger brothers and sisters, towering over their older siblings. Then you know."

"Know what?"

"You know they got here around the age of the tallest child."

"That's just stupid, Jolene, height is dictated by a person's genetics."

"When kids get fed enough, they reach their

genetic potential. They got to be fed enough, first, in order to reach that genetic potential. The ones that don't get fed, don't get as tall. It's plain biology, Connie."

Connie opened her mouth, looking as if she was trying to say something, but nothing came out. Jolene understood, she didn't know where terms like, *genetic potential* were coming from, either. "Listen here, if your kids were starving, wouldn't you do anything you could to feed them?"

Connie nodded.

"That's right, you and all your church ladies are the lucky ones. And you-all pray to Christ, right?"

Connie nodded, again.

"Well, if I remember right, didn't Jesus say to help your neighbor as yourself if you want to enter the kingdom of heaven?"

"Yeah, that's right. That's what he said."

"Well, good, you remember it, too. So, maybe you and all your lady friends could use some of that Christianity you're always parading around and give

Lady Guadalupe and the Sno-Kone Hut

the unfortunates a hand up. You know? Like Jesus said to?"

Evelyn toddled back, oblivious to Connie's outraged expression and Jolene's calm one.

"Here are two fifties and we can change the hundred back for fifties tomorrow." Evelyn smiled. Jolene smiled a genuine smile back at the old lady.

Connie counted out the change and made not another sound, foregoing having the last word. A first in Jolene's experience.

Jolene gathered up the bills Connie slapped down and left.

The sun was setting, and she thought about making her way to Leon's, but the new skirt swished in a nice way. She liked how it fluttered in the slight breeze, and decided a long walk home, by herself, would suit just fine. After the crowds of people she'd been dealing with, being alone was welcome.

Mateo came to see her every day. Despite the crush of work, when he'd come behind the counter and hold her hand, she'd stop whatever she was doing and listen.

It wasn't that either of them were all that interested in what the teacher said that day, or what they had for lunch, or how the cafeteria ladies touched him for luck. It was only all he knew to talk about, and he needed to talk to her and hold her hand. Jolene believed she needed it, too.

Being part of all that mystery and power was nearly too much for them, but together they'd taken her in and allowed the Lady to change them. Jolene pulled Lady Guadalupe out of her pocket and held it in her hand as she walked.

*But how am I different?* Standing up to Connie Plunkett, without resorting to throwing a punch, was different. Jolene chuckled, remembering grade-school when she'd gotten in a few good licks before a teacher intervened.

She hadn't walked through town since getting her driver's license, and wearing a skirt to boot, all sorts

Lady Guadalupe and the Sno-Kone Hut

of things were different. Jolene swung her arms and hummed a sort of tune while making her way through the park. Soon she was on the long stretch of road lined by houses that led to River Road.

"Hey there, Jolene."

Pulled up to the curb behind her was Lyman, in his silent, electric car. She didn't know if it was seeing him so unexpectedly surprising her the most, or the fact of him talking to her that near town, in broad daylight, where anyone could see them. "Hey, there, Lyman."

"Need a lift?"

*Did she?* Jolene looked down, wondering if maybe, after working so many hours straight, she could use a ride after all. She sighed. "Sure, thanks," and went to the other side of his car and got in.

"Fasten your seat belt, young lady." Lyman smiled as if they did this all the time. "What were you doing in town?" he asked, pulling away.

"Getting out of Dodge for a while."

"I saw you on the TV last night and all the stuff

going on at your place. I tried to call, but you never answered."

A van from the Richmond TV station had come and embarrassed her no end with a bunch of stupid questions she'd refused to answer. Leon had come to her rescue and looking like the dignified church deacon he was, explained the goings on at the campground.

"They called you, *a local healer*."

"I know." Jolene looked at her lap. "I've had more calls for readings and had to put them all off, too."

"I guess Leon's running the place while you're taking a break?"

"Naw, he's gone, too. We closed up." Jolene had an odd sensation running around in her, something like fear and sadness all mixed together into one tight bunch. She clutched Lady Guadalupe tighter and felt the unease lift some.

"What about…"

"Everyone left. Lady Guadalupe rose up out of the river like a mist and drifted upstream."

Lady Guadalupe and the Sno-Kone Hut

Lyman was silent, frowning. "That didn't *really* happen, did it?"

"Yep, it did." Jolene sighed again and looked out the window at weeds blooming with bright yellow flowers.

"You look real nice there, Jolene."

She was aware of him glancing at her profile, taking in the rise and fall of her breasts, the dark ringlets around her face, and the pretty outfit. "I have to say I was surprised," she said, turning to catch him looking.

"By what?"

"You, stopping for me." They were almost to the bridge.

"Why? I was leaving work and saw you. I wasn't sure it was you at first, I don't think I ever saw you in a long skirt before."

"Is that why you stopped?"

Lyman reddened but said nothing.

"I asked, is that why you stopped?"

"No, that is not why I stopped."

Sighing, she stared out the window again. The cold air-conditioning was annoying, blowing on one spot on her arm and making the car feel closed off from the world. Without asking, she turned it off and pushed the button that rolled down the window. The warm breeze felt nice on her naked shoulders. Jolene almost felt like Scarlett O'Hara and was glad more of her unease was blowing away too.

"I stopped because I'm nearly a free man."

His voice was shaky sounding. Jolene's curiosity was aroused. "Free of what, Lyman?"

He shook his head. "Of being conventional, having to do things certain ways, being careful all the time."

"What in the world are you getting ready to do? Quit your job? What about your place in the community?"

"I'm done with it," came out sharp and fast.

Lyman sounded so different he might as well

Lady Guadalupe and the Sno-Kone Hut have been someone else altogether. "What's going on, Lyman?"

He didn't answer, only gripped the steering wheel more tightly and said, "Oh, to hell with it, I've got to tell someone." Lyman got to the other side of the bridge and pulled his car off the road. He unfastened his seatbelt and got out. She watched him remove his coat and tie, wondering what old Lyman was up to this time and wondering if he realized he'd said, "hell."

He threw the jacket and tie in the back, then returned to the driver's seat. With the collar of his light-blue shirt unbuttoned and his face so relaxed she almost didn't recognize him, he turned towards her and smiled like they were the best of friends. Gone was his awkwardness, his hesitancy. He was as graceful, and beautiful as any of God's creatures, and in that singular moment Jolene fell smack dab in love with a guy she'd known her entire life.

"What I did, Jolene, wasn't exactly right in the eyes of the law, but no one," he looked serious, almost like a child trying to appear grown-up and Jolene suppressed a giggle. "I promise you, *no one* will be hurt by what I did."

It was a little scary to recognize how irreversible love was. She hadn't known about that part of it before.

"And, now I'm close to the end of all this stuff, almost free of this town that makes life like living in a straight-jacket."

Jolene was reeling, but not ready to let Lyman know. She was sure the smile on her face looked fake, but it was the best she could come up with. Still, "What'd you do there Lyman?"

He grinned. "I came across some information about a new distribution center last year."

"So?"

"I bought the land they want to build it on, out on Route Five where the Sno-Kone Hut is?"

"So?" Long ago, Jolene's daddy told her the farmer who owned the property slapped the large plywood snow-cone on an outbuilding by the road

Lady Guadalupe and the Sno-Kone Hut
and started a new business that didn't take. All that remained was the snow-cone, paint peeling from its once pink top, with, *Sno-Kone Hut*, printed in faded, but still visible letters, on the side of the building.

"I've been in negotiations with them, and we're almost there, almost signing on the dotted line."

"I guess that's good."

"Good? It's great is what it is." Lyman leaned his head back through the open window. "Man, it's a pretty day." He sat straighter. "Almost as pretty as you."

She felt her cheeks burn and hoped he didn't notice. She wasn't sure how to begin telling him she loved him. She was still figuring out what it meant.

"When this is all over, I'm thinking you and me will be taking a cruise somewhere."

In her mind's eye she visualized them, smelled the salt air and noted the easy access to a bedroom. "That sounds real nice, Lyman."

"I didn't have enough money, so I made myself a loan."

"For the cruise?"

Lyman laughed, shook his head. "No, for the land. I used all my savings, cashed in my investments, but it wasn't enough. I needed some collateral, so I used my mother's house. As soon as I pay that off, you and me are gonna do some traveling." He smiled.

"You did what?" *Crap. She was in love with a man who'd steal from his own mother.*

"But it will be okay, Jolene. I promise. I'll be selling the property in probably a week or two. Then it's all over. I'll pay off the loan and make enough on this one deal to retire."

His excitement demanded some sort of response, but Jolene couldn't think of one.

"I can't wait, Jolene. We can travel, do any damn thing we want."

"What about the store?"

"Let Leon handle things for a while, or his son, that Jack guy."

*How had she'd kept her feelings for him hidden*

## Lady Guadalupe and the Sno-Kone Hut

*so long?* She loved hearing him say "we" and knowing he meant him and her, but there was still the problem of his tarot reading, using inside information and putting a mortgage on his mother's property. *I was his goal, his reason for committing a crime.*

Yet, there were other forces at play too. Like Magnolia being a place where people felt bound to act exactly the way Lyman did – paranoid and stupid. But he was wrong, dead wrong.

He could have had her right then and there and for the rest of his life. He didn't need money, or to leave town to have her. Hell, she'd even marry him if he wanted. All he had to do was stop giving a shit about what everyone else thought, and their lives would be wonderful.

Lyman didn't see the freedom floating all around him, right in front of his eyes. It made her feel sorry for the short-sighted man she loved and awkwardly, she patted his arm while resisting an urge to press his head to her breasts, hug and kiss him.

Lyman smiled like they'd settled something. He turned and fastened his seat belt, then started the car. They were back on the road with Jolene wondering how in the world it would all end. Lyman in jail? If he didn't learn humility and concern for others, he might. She sure didn't need him in jail. Jolene glanced at his profile and wished with everything in her she could have had a least a couple of days to enjoy him, before having to go to work on saving his sorry ass.

She shook her head. *How am I going to get at the good man lost inside all the crap he believes?* She didn't know, but she was going to have to find out and find out fast.

"I thought we could go to Martinsboro tonight, go to that new Italian place. What do you think?"

Jolene's head whipped left, her eyebrows raised. "Tonight? Like right this minute?"

"Yeah, why not? I think we could both use a night away from here."

She turned to face the windshield. "Okay, why

Lady Guadalupe and the Sno-Kone Hut

not?"

She glanced at the new love of her life, almost frightened by the change in him. "You sure are acting different, Lyman. I don't know if I've ever seen you like this."

"This is me happy, sweetheart, just me being happy." Then he chuckled and slapped her thigh playfully. "Something I haven't been in a long, long time."

*Had he somehow sensed she'd fallen in love with him? Was that why he was so relaxed, so attractive? Or had she fallen in love because he'd already changed, gotten happy from all his illicit dealings?* Jolene didn't know and worrying only made the questions murkier.

She stared out the window, missing her granny something awful. *What do you do, Granny, when the man you're given to ain't always on the up-and-up?*

Granny had loved her son, her only child, with a vengeance at times. She taught Jolene love had two sides, soft and hard, and people made mistakes not knowing it. Granny pointed out people who were unbalanced in love, mostly women, thinking love was only its soft side. The new wife who kept her philandering husband. The much older, much bitterer wife, who'd done the same.

Love, Granny told her, changed folks, and it was the only thing that did. That was the price of love, letting it change you. It's how mothers could lift a car up off a child. That was the hard part of love, doing hard things because you loved someone and not expecting nothing back.

When Jolene's daddy came home from a binge, worn out and ragged, her granny would feed him, put him to bed and not pay him much mind until he was sobered and rested enough to be very hung-over. That's when she'd set Jolene down nearby and say in a way Lincoln Gibson would be unable to avoid hearing, "Your daddy is sick right now from the booze 'cause he's had himself an attack of selfishness. The

Lady Guadalupe and the Sno-Kone Hut

whole time he was out pouring poison into his body, he weren't thinking about you, or me. He weren't no daddy, or son a'tall, to no one."

Granny would always add something like, "Now the man thinks he's going to resume living in this family and start being a son and daddy again, and *I'm* saying that ain't gonna happen unless he sets things right first."

"Now this child, Lincoln," Granny would point to Jolene, "has already lost a mother, and you just disappearing like you did is sure to have hit a soft spot in her where parents are supposed to be."

Then Granny would make Jolene tell her daddy exactly how she felt and Granny would do the same. Sometimes Daddy would cry, but Granny wouldn't let his tears interrupt whatever had to be said.

When Jolene was little, she'd hated those times. All she wanted to do was crawl in her daddy's lap and let him pet her hair. But Granny would insist she tell her daddy how scared she was and Jolene would, but not like Granny very much afterwards. When Jolene was a teenager and understood the burden he placed on Granny and Lorraine, trying to run things by themselves, she didn't have any trouble chewing him out.

Once Granny exhausted the subject of how her son's actions had hurt his family, he would apologize, say he didn't know what got into him at times and life would resume. Until the next time.

Jolene's daddy had been one of the last draftees to Vietnam, an unlucky lottery number caught him in the war's dying net. Granny said his demons came from those days and there weren't no cure she could find for it.

"Lyman?"

"Yeah?"

"I'm too tired to drive all the way to Martinsboro tonight. I've been putting in a lot of hours lately, with the vision and stuff."

He looked disappointed. "You want me to take

Lady Guadalupe and the Sno-Kone Hut
you home?"

Jolene sighed. "Yeah, I'm not much company tonight. I'm just too tired."

The place had cleared out by the time Lyman pulled his car behind the Bait & Tackle. A few abandoned cars were scattered out front and in the pasture, but the place felt empty. Jolene wasn't even sure any residents were in their trailers, none of the usual sounds of music, or TV came from the campground.

The quiet felt odd when she stepped from the car. A heron, who, with his wife, claimed Jolene's riverfront as their territory, rose up from a nearby tree, clacking at the humans for disturbing his peace.

Jolene looked at Lyman. "I can't offer you anything to eat, ain't nothing left. I might could find a cold beer, or two if you'd like."

He smiled the same relaxed, handsome smile he'd had on his face since they'd crossed the bridge. "That'd be great."

"I'll get them, we can walk down to the river, and I'll show you where Lady Guadalupe came up." Lyman's face fell, but she pretended not to notice. Soon she was back, coming from the screened-in porch with two green bottles in her hand.

They walked to the river holding hands like high-school kids. She took him to the pier by the fish house where they sat on the rough planks overlooking the river, swinging their legs over the side.

Jolene pointed to a place on the water. "That's where Mateo drowned. He saw the Lady then, and after Jackson and I brought him around, I saw her too."

"How?"

"In the child's eyes, just as plain as day." Jolene took a swig of beer.

"Oh," Lyman sounded relieved, "you didn't *see* her, see her. It was more like a vision?"

Jolene started to get riled and then remembered she loved the man. She waited to feel the Lady's peace return, and when it did, she sighed. "Yeah, she was like

Lady Guadalupe and the Sno-Kone Hut

a vision."

"It's nice, all quiet and empty this way."

"I love you."

"You what?" Lyman stared at Jolene, wide-eyed.

"You heard me."

"You love me? Since when?"

"Since when you picked me up."

"Are you telling me before I picked you up, you didn't love me, and afterwards you did?"

Jolene shook her head. "Naw, I've probably loved you for some time, just didn't want to know it."

"Why not?"

"Cause when you love someone you're given to that person."

"I don't understand."

"When you told me you loved me, didn't you give yourself to me?"

Lyman sat straighter, furrowing his brow. "Well, yeah, I guess. I'm sure not interested in anyone else."

"I guess, maybe I wasn't so sure about that part

of it."

He smiled. "So you don't want anyone but me?"

"I haven't in a long, long time." Jolene smiled shyly back.

"Wow, I can't believe it. What a great day. I mean, this has been an unbelievably great day." He bent to kiss her.

Soon, Jolene found herself hiking up that yellow skirt with the blue flowers, right there on those rough boards. Even when caught up in the act of loving, Jolene was struck by the knowledge it wouldn't have mattered if a crowd of people had been standing around, staring, the urge to unite with Lyman was that strong.

And Lyman appeared to be similarly possessed by the same need.

It was easier that time to become one creature, to move into the sacred space where boundaries disappeared, just like Granny said would happen when people gave themselves to each other.

Lady Guadalupe and the Sno-Kone Hut

Jolene had thought Granny crazy for a long, long time, or maybe just very lucky after finding Grandpa, but after kissing Lyman one last, sweet kiss when their lovemaking was done, Jolene was only glad to have at last joined Granny's ranks.

Jolene and Lyman were in various states of being undressed. He still wore the blue starched shirt, unbuttoned and nothing else. Jolene's skirt was wadded around her waist and everything else scattered on the pier.

"Would you like to go swimming? Is the water warm enough?" Lyman asked.

"Oh, yes, that sounds real nice."

They wore underwear in case any residents happened to spy them and went down the steps to the beach. The sun was setting, but it was still light out. The water was colder than Jolene had thought, and she gasped when swimming out.

Lyman gingerly went to where the water hit his knees. "Maybe this isn't such a good idea."

"It's a wonderful idea, come on in."

"My dick's going to shrink, and you're going to think I have a little, tiny dick."

"I already know how big your dick is, come on, city boy." Jolene laughed.

With a whoop, Lyman dove and swam out.

"You'll get used to it in a while," she said.

They grinned and treaded water. Jolene had lured Lyman to the same spot Mateo had drowned, hoping the lingering effects of the Lady would help him. He shook his head, swinging the hair from his face in a gesture she remembered from school days.

"You ready to get out?" he asked.

"Sure thing."

They went back to the fish house, gathered up their clothes off the pier and Lyman put his shirt over his wet boxers. "What are you, Jolene?"

"Huh?" she asked, slipping on her skirt.

"I mean, what nationality are you?"

Jolene ducked her head. "Don't rightly know."

Lady Guadalupe and the Sno-Kone Hut

He touched her hair, wet and curling. "You and your family have such distinctive looks."

Jolene looked into Lyman's eyes. "Granny said we was Portuguese, mixed up with Indian tribes."

"From where?"

"Well, I guess, from Portugal, by way of South America. Granny said by the time settlers got to the Appalachians, my people had been there for over two-hundred years."

Lyman took Jolene's hand. They walked towards the ramp that led to the dirt path to her house. "Really?"

"That's what she told me."

"When did your family come to Magnolia?"

"Late eighteen hundreds, when Great-Great-Granddaddy Gibson won this place in a poker game."

"So, you're Portuguese and Indian?"

"That's what Granny and Great-Aunt Mabel told me, but I got something to show you."

Jolene led him through the screened-in porch,

flipping on the kitchen light and going to the large, glass-fronted cabinet. She opened the far left, bottom drawer, pulled out a brown cardboard folder and placed it on the kitchen table. She opened the folder like a book.

"Don't look like no kinda Portuguese I've ever seen," Jolene said dourly, looking down.

Lyman looked over her shoulder at an ancient sepia photograph of a family, at roughly the turn of the previous century. The father, a dark-skinned man with oddly light eyes and straight black hair, wearing a mustache and somber expression, was flanked by his dark-skinned, dark-eyed wife and three young children. One child was pale, the other two dark, all with curly, dark hair and those strangely light eyes.

"Them's my great, great, great, grandparents and that," Jolene pointed to a dark-faced baby in the woman's lap, "was Granny's great-grandfather."

"Wow," Lyman said. "We don't have any photographs of family that old."

Lady Guadalupe and the Sno-Kone Hut

"All I can say is Granny insisted we were Portuguese and Indian and she wouldn't budge none from it. I've always thought there was more to the story, but can't say for sure what it might be. Daddy once told me we was called Melungeons, but he made me promise never to tell Granny I knew the word."

"Melungeons?"

"Yeah, we were setting trot-lines for catfish late one night, nobody around and he whispered the word like he was scared of it. When I asked him what it meant, he said all he knew was when those settlers came to the Appalachians, they called us Melungeons, even though we spoke the same language as them."

"Doesn't matter." Lyman pulled Jolene to him, wrapping his arms around her and hugging her. "The only thing that matters is you love me too."

"Well, then, you gotta quit hiding me."

Lyman stood straighter, but before he could get into his stubbornness, Jolene stood on her tiptoes and kissed him. When she got him to kissing her back, she pulled him to the couch and set him down. "I can't go on like this."

Lyman started to interrupt, but Jolene waved her hand and sat next to him. "Let me finish. I know this ain't a one-way street, I got to do some changing, too." She sat silent for a moment, staring intp his eyes. "Being two people who love each other changes things."

Lyman smiled, took a deep breath and let it out. "It is so nice to hear you say it. I think you're going to have to say it a whole lot, just to make up for all the times I said it by myself."

Jolene smiled too. "Maybe, but now that you know everything there is to know about me, you gotta decide if you're gonna claim me or not."

"Claim you?"

"I want to tell everyone I know I'm in love with Lyman Pettigrew. I want you to want to do that too."

"But Jolene, I'm so close. A couple of weeks is all I need. Then I'm free, I told you."

Lady Guadalupe and the Sno-Kone Hut

"All that stuff you're doing?"

"Yeah?"

"Remember your reading, being corrupt, doing the wrong things? It's not gonna work out, Lyman, if you don't change."

"What do you mean?" he bristled.

Jolene knew she'd lost him and didn't know what else to say. Exhaustion settled on her, heavy, weighing her down and she was too tired to think. She sighed. "I'll keep us a secret for a while, if that's what you want, but don't say I didn't warn you."

Lyman looked relieved. "I know you believe in all that stuff, but I swear, Jolene, everything is going just as planned. I'm sorry as hell I did that reading. I'm sorry it got you all worked up, but look here, I'm not worried at all. I *know* in a couple of weeks, we can do anything we want."

She shook her head. "Whatever. I'm really tired, I think I'll turn in early. Maybe you'd better go get something to eat."

"Sure you won't come?"

"Yeah, I'm bushed."

"How about us taking a weekend away, go to Nags Head, or somewhere?"

"That'd be nice."

Lyman half rose. "Okay then." He kissed the top of her head and stood. "Maybe I can come around tomorrow night?"

"Sure."

He seemed uncertain. "I'll call around six?"

"That'd be fine."

Lyman pulled khaki slacks over his damp boxers and tucked in his shirt. "You okay?" he asked, coming back to the couch with his shoes and socks.

Jolene thought for a moment, smoothing out the quilt on the back of the couch. "I'm worried about you, big time worried. I *do* believe in the readings and *have* seen too much truth in them to doubt it."

Lyman froze with one shoe in his hand. "I think it will turn out fine. I don't have any reason not to think

# Lady Guadalupe and the Sno-Kone Hut

so."

She looked him dead in the eye. "If I'm the only one worried about you, Lyman, so be it."

Lyman's laugh sounded empty, self-conscious. "I'll be fine, we'll be fine, quit worrying."

"Wish that were possible." Jolene sighed, stood up and walked him out the screened-porch door.

He kissed her again and loped off to his car.

Jolene waved as he pulled out, went back inside and gave her home and the store a good sage-cleaning. She fingered the ancient envelope that held the fragments of a red ribbon. Lyman Pettigrew would never know, but at some point the following night, a tiny scrap of red regret would be glued to the inside toe of his left tasseled loafer.

Chapter Nine

It was still early, yet already a day of wonder. Connie Plunkett sat on Granny's green painted, arrow-backed chair like it was nothing at all for her to be there, asking for a reading. Connie's eyes were closed and thoughts crossed her face like ripples on a river. She was supposed to state her question, and it looked like she was having as much trouble coming up with one as Lyman.

Jolene's chairs and kitchen table were a patchwork of greens, the lightest, softest green being topmost while other, deeper shades of green and wood peeked out where spots of paint had been knocked off.

The last time they'd been painted was when she was around sixteen. Granny got her to finish the job by

Lady Guadalupe and the Sno-Kone Hut

hiding the keys to the truck until she was done. Granny was always trying to spruce the place up with paint and a washrag. Jolene felt it was a shame she didn't take after her granny more.

But, very weird this; Connie acted like she didn't care at all how shabby Jolene had let the place get. Jolene sat across from a woman so different from the person she'd known her entire life. Connie was nearly a stranger.

"That thing out on Route Five?"

Jolene jumped when Connie spoke, but, thankfully, Connie's eyes were still closed. Jolene hated the idea of even this new version of Connie seeing her vulnerable. "You mean Lady Guadalupe?"

Connie's eyes flew open. "Do you think it's real, or some kind of hallucination?" she demanded, her eyes wide. Jolene knew things in Connie's home had become unglued. She worried how unglued Connie might be as a result.

Connie's stare felt uncomfortable. *I am so*

*tired of all the intensity from everyone I come across anymore.* "They say not everyone can see her," Jolene stated bluntly as she folded her arms across her chest.

"I saw her and wish I hadn't." Connie looked down, locked in some private hell.

The small-town rumor-mill had had a field day with Connie's husband admitting to being gay and leaving town to live with some young man in Richmond.

Granny had instructed Jolene in how to use her voice, put emotion in it and throw it from the corner of the room to startle folks awake. Jolene was good at it. "Why's that Connie?"

Connie snapped, anger curling her lip, making her ugly. "Because I saw it and it changed me. I can't get it out of my head. It messed me up bad, did something to me."

*Lord, she's touchy.* Jolene kept her voice gentle and ditched the voice tricks. She was curious as hell to find out how Connie, Queen Bee of Magnolia,

Lady Guadalupe and the Sno-Kone Hut was messed up. "Most people who saw the Lady, me included, found the experience comforting."

"Comforting?" Connie said sarcastically, in the cold way Jolene knew so well.

But since Jolene had been touched by Lady Guadalupe, all she could see was one, very miserable woman. "Yes, Connie, comforting."

Connie couldn't keep it up. She crumpled around the edges, growing soft. "Maybe. It's... just... now... everything... is sooooo messed up." Connie's head sunk to the table and she wailed.

This was *not* the Connie Plunkett Jolene had known her entire life. Suddenly, it was important to remember Connie always being the one to invite everyone, but Jolene, to every birthday party she had. It was important to recollect the names Connie called her, like "dirty girl" because of her dusky skin and "slut" when boys began noticing.

Sometimes, it was like Granny's voice still lived, Jolene nearly able to hear, "Act right 'cause this woman *is* a paying customer."

*I guess I could pat her on the arm, say some damn soothing thing, but honestly, why?* Jolene silently argued back.

She sat with folded arms and waited. Connie had already paid for the hour, if all she wanted to do with it was cry, well, that was fine. And, for a while, that's what Connie did, until she began to wind-down like an old clock, hiccupping and wiping her face on her shirt sleeves. She blushed when she raised her head.

*What a day, Connie embarrassed in front of me, will wonders never cease?*

"I know I don't deserve any pity from you." Connie's eyes were clear and determined.

Jolene hated the shivers of fear running down her spine. "We were never close," she replied.

"No, it was more than that. I was ugly to you. I admit it. I'm sorry, Jolene. I am."

She wasn't joking, one look in the woman's fierce eyes told Jolene everything. It was the same look

Lady Guadalupe and the Sno-Kone Hut which had reduced more than one girl to tears, but now, magically, turned around to doing some good.

Jolene considered her old nemesis, her expression blank as she considered the notion of letting go of this part of her past. She recalled walking home after school, making up what she called "happy stories" she could tell Granny about her day, and how every school-day morning was an absolute misery because of the woman in front of her and the others like her.

Glancing at the clock, Jolene got up, wet a clean dishtowel, brought it to Connie and placed the towel on the back of Connie's neck.

"Oh, my." Connie's hands went over Jolene's. "That feels wonderful."

Jolene felt a sudden kinship with Connie that seemed downright disrespectful to her own self. Granny's advice crossed her thoughts a second time, *you got to keep yourself apart from them. Don't let them take you over in any way, good or bad. Respect the cards, and you cain't never go wrong.*

Jolene took a deep breath and sat. "We have time to do a short reading if you want."

Connie looked up from wiping her shiny, red face with the towel.

Jolene shrugged her shoulders. "You still want one?"

Connie nodded, slowly.

The cards were unwrapped the way Granny taught. "So what's your question?"

"Um." Connie cleared her throat. "I don't know how to put it in words." Frown lines creased her forehead.

"Just say it any old way, and I'll help you with the rest." Jolene shuffled the cards, focusing on the running water sound they made. She took another deep breath. Granny was right again – trust the cards.

"Should I take my husband up on his suggestion?"

"What did he suggest?" Jolene didn't look up or stop shuffling. Sometimes the cards were like engines,

Lady Guadalupe and the Sno-Kone Hut powering everything around them.

Connie hesitated, and sounding like she'd decided something, said, "That we sell everything."

"Why does he want to do that?"

"He thinks we'd all be better off if I took the kids, left Magnolia and started over somewhere else."

Jolene had to ask, "Together?"

Connie's cheeks turned a deeper red. "Not together, but in the same place, in Richmond. He wants to be a father to the kids, he wants to support me in whatever I want, except he can't keep pretending to be someone he isn't. He says he can't stand to lie anymore."

*I know how he feels.* "What do *you* want to do?"

Connie stared at the ceiling, tears sliding down her face. "I don't know. I've never lived anywhere but here. Living somewhere else feels wrong. No one would know me. I wouldn't know anyone." She looked at Jolene. "He won't stay, and he could make me sell the house as part of the divorce anyway. But he says he won't. He says it's up to me."

"So your question is, should I go away with my former husband, or stay here in Magnolia, right?"

"I guess so, sounds simple when you say it." Connie was exhausted, her face haggard and desperate.

Jolene didn't know how simple any of this was going to be, but she had a strong feeling the cards were going to help Connie, help her a lot.

"What we're gonna do here is a horseshoe reading." Jolene handed Connie the deck. "Say your question and cut the cards three times."

Connie sat up straighter and held the cards, looking at them curiously. "Should I stay here and change nothing, or leave and change everything?" She cut the deck three times and handed the cards to Jolene with surprise in her eyes.

Jolene had seen that look before when the cards helped some troubled soul get their thoughts together. Connie suddenly looked better, stronger, like she knew what she was doing.

Lady Guadalupe and the Sno-Kone Hut

Jolene spread the cards in a fan. "Pick seven and hand them to me."

Connie did. Jolene stacked the cards first to last, then placed them in a horseshoe pattern. The first card surprised. Not often did answers come so soon, or so clearly. "This card represents your question, and you have the Knight of Cups here. This signifies a proposal, usually from a man, who is sincere and caring."

"For real?"

"Yes, for real."

"He *is* different, Jolene." Connie's face lit up as she spoke. "He's as kind, as kind can be. He does anything he can to make this whole thing easier for me and the kids. What bothers me is…" Connie blushed and cast her eyes on her lap.

Jolene waited. The cards were in charge.

"If I hadn't seen Lady Guadalupe, or whatever she is," Connie started slowly. "I wouldn't have cared at all what he did, and I know it. All I would have cared about was my reputation and how I was going to make him pay for disgracing me. That's what's messing me up. I keep seeing how I would have been." Her eyes searched Jolene's, looking for some sort of response.

"It's a lot when you see yourself. I know exactly what you mean." Jolene nodded encouragingly

Connie took another deep breath, seeming to consider things, then spoke soft and fast. "Even when Momma asked me to do something as simple as bring down their winter clothes, all I could see was how I *would* have done it before, resentfully. I would have told everyone I knew about how helpless poor old Momma and Daddy were getting, saying all of it in some sort of casual way so everyone would think what a wonderful daughter I was." She was out of breath. Her eyes asked if that was okay.

Jolene said gently, "Most people don't see so much about themselves until they are real old, Connie, if then. Being able to see yourself the way others do is a good thing." She waited for a response, and after Connie sat silent, she added, "I mean what I'm saying.

Lady Guadalupe and the Sno-Kone Hut

I've had some experiences with that myself lately and for the same, exact reason. Lady Guadalupe opened my eyes, too."

Jolene watched confusion take over Connie's features – a wrinkling of her brow, a tilt of her head. Connie might take her words as an insult, or as support and Jolene couldn't tell which way the wind was blowing. "I saw Lady Guadalupe with the Mexican boy, Mateo, the one that almost drowned?"

Connie nodded.

"He saw her first. Then I saw her. She changed both of us. I know what you're going through. It gets easier after a while."

Exhaustion registered on Connie's face. "God, I hope so. It's been a week, and it's only getting worse. That's why I had to come see you."

Jolene looked at the cards. "Sounds like it's Richard, who's sincere and caring and making you a proposal."

"Yeah, I think so, keep going, what's next?"

Connie looked ready.

Jolene flipped the next card. "This is your present condition. You are someone who can create a new life with the wisdom you've gained from the lessons you've learned."

Connie nodded again, understanding.

The next card was flipped. "The Six of Wands is a great message. You'll be recognized for your talents and abilities, promoted in some manner, maybe related to working, or not."

"So what does it mean?"

"I can't tell you how it will play itself out, only that your fears don't hold water. In the end, you will be honored, not disrespected." Jolene turned over the next card and was again surprised. "The Page of Swords represents any obstacles facing you here. All I can say is there ain't any."

"No obstacles?"

"Not with this. This card says it's time to go out there and make your own unforgettable mark on the

Lady Guadalupe and the Sno-Kone Hut

world in your own way." Jolene was smiling.

"Is this a good reading, Jolene?"

"A very good reading, the best I done in a long while." They grinned at each other like old friends.

The next card was the Queen of Wands, another good omen. "This has to do with other people's opinions about you and what you are doing, and I think it means this is the woman you are becoming. You will be seen as a good woman, warm, generous and welcoming, with an air of sophistication and strength. You will not have to worry about having your needs met."

"I would love to be that person." Connie sounded shy.

"I think that person is who you truly are." Jolene surprised herself by saying.

She turned over the next to last card, and the joy around them evaporated. It was the Devil.

"This is the influence around you right now and it ain't good." Their eyes met. "Is someone trying to dominate you right now, tell you what to do?"

"My momma."

"Is she pressuring you to do anything in particular?"

Connie regained the agitated, desperate expression on her face. "Momma caught wind we might move. She says I can't leave. But the kids are getting picked on at school, and when I tell her, she doesn't seem to care very much. So there's that, and of course, Pastor Barnes stopped by with Aunt Norma."

"What did *they* want?"

"I'm sure he was only trying to help." Connie looked beaten. "Norma only likes to stick her nose in my business."

"This card says someone around you is power hungry. It could be your mother, aunt, pastor, or all of them. It's important for you to not anger or irritate anyone who shows signs of hostility. If you do, you will unleash a devil in them, and there is no limit to the amount of havoc a devil can create. Walk away; don't

Lady Guadalupe and the Sno-Kone Hut confront. That's what this is saying."

"But the pastor, he's the furthest thing from a devil, isn't he?"

"Trust me." Jolene cast her voice low, so Connie would hear it. "The devil wears religion's clothes a lot more often than the garb of a sinner." Which was a direct quote from Granny. "Granny said most preachers were ignorant of spirit and the ones that did, were often corrupted by it."

"My aunt *was* rather pushy."

"What does she want you to do?"

Connie tossed back a lock of hair. "She wanted me to know my place was here in Magnolia, with my family's support around me."

"What did Pastor Barnes have to say?"

"That it wasn't my fault if my husband misrepresented himself, the divorce would be forgiven, but you know what, Jolene?"

"What?"

"He was so cut and dried about it, like that was

my only choice. It didn't seem like he really cared how I felt, only that I was supposed to listen to him and do the right thing."

"I know the type." *And you used to be included in the bunch.* Jolene smiled to herself. "What else are you supposed to do?"

"Get more involved in the church, stay busy, keep the kids away from Richard as much as possible, because he's living a *sinful* life, stuff like that."

"Stay away from people who want to control you. This is a clear warning. But don't make them angry either."

"You know, that kind of crap gets me in my softest place."

"What do you mean?"

"I know I used to throw my weight around, pull strings and stuff, but," Connie looked around the room, tears in her eyes, "but mostly I knew I wasn't the brightest light bulb in the box."

"I don't understand."

Lady Guadalupe and the Sno-Kone Hut

"School, Jolene. School was hard for me."

"How? You were always on the honor roll, you even went to college."

Connie was like a much older woman when she spoke. "You have no idea how hard I worked to keep those grades." She looked down. "No idea."

Jolene sat straighter. "No, I guess I didn't. I always thought of you as one of the smart kids. I think everybody did."

Connie sat straighter too. "No, probably only the hardest working kid you knew."

"So, I'm still not making the connection here. What does that have to do with this being hard?"

"Because I think people like Momma, my pastor, and aunt, are people who know better than me and I *should* listen to them." Tears welled and spilled down her face. She wiped them roughly on her sleeve.

"Who in the world would know better what feels right to you, than you?" Jolene leaned over the table, speaking gently. "Especially when nobody else cares *how* you feel, you'd better be ready to do that for yourself, don't you think?"

"All I can see lately is how, even if Richard only married me to hide who he really was, I married him for the same reasons."

Jolene wasn't sure what Connie was getting ready to confess and kept her silence.

"I used him too, for his paycheck, the nice house, the country club, all of it. I was sick of trying to keep up at school and ended up no better than a prostitute. Probably the only difference between me and them was, I was just more calculating." Connie stared at the cards with a bleak expression.

Jolene spotted the burned spots along the table's edge in front of Connie. They were from where her daddy used to set his lit cigarettes and probably why she'd never wanted to paint the table again. "You ain't no different than most of the married women in this town, Connie, except for the figuring it out part."

Connie had the same quizzical expression on

Lady Guadalupe and the Sno-Kone Hut

her face she'd had earlier, but this time Jolene laughed, knowing she didn't have to fear Connie's wrath anymore.

"Oh, my, gosh." Connie bolted upright and looked Jolene straight in the eye. "I'm gonna move." A big grin came over her face. It was like watching a doll become animated, coming alive. "It's going to be good for all of us, me, the kids will be so happy to leave, and Richard will be thrilled we'll all be in the same town. We can re-design our family our own way, can't we?"

"Yes, Connie, you can. You will all be fine."

Jolene turned over the last card and smiled. Now, officially, this was one of the most positive readings she'd given in a long time. "The Eight of Wands is the outcome, Connie. Love is coming, sexual love, pretty soon you're gonna have some good lovin' in your life."

Tears streamed down her face. "Really? Why? I don't deserve anything like that."

"Doesn't matter. Love's in your forecast and

there ain't nothing you can do about it. There's more too."

"Oh Lord, I don't know if I can take any more."

"Some other positive changes, like a wonderful opportunity doing something you love and moving to where you will find happiness. This is a great reading, Connie."

"Thank you, Jolene, thank you so much."

"Thank the spirits. I'm only the reporter." Jolene liked the airy feeling her home got after a good reading. Connie stood stiffly, and they went to the front of the store. She hugged Jolene.

Jolene hugged her back, sensing camaraderie between them like soldiers who'd won a battle. She took down the "Closed for Dinner" sign and opened the door. The bell overhead rang out more cheerfully than usual.

Connie hesitated at the doorway, like she intended to leave, but had a change of heart. She turned around. "You need to go out there on Route Five."

Lady Guadalupe and the Sno-Kone Hut

"See the Lady again?"

"Yes, see her again."

Connie was giving her a hard look like she meant this. The change in the woman was dramatic. *I wonder if the cards are talking to me, through Connie.* "Okay. Sure thing. I will," she stammered.

Connie nodded slowly. "It's important you do, Jolene. Don't forget."

"I won't," Jolene said and smiled as the dark-haired woman walked to her car. It was odd, was all, meeting such a different Connie, yet still hearing plenty of that same old, bossy person in her voice.

## Chapter Ten

It was a few busy hours later, right after Jackson arrived and took over when Lyman's car pulled around back. She'd agreed to try the new place Martinsboro, a forty-five minute drive away and go to a movie afterward.

Jolene's stomach clenched, she was sick of feeling like it was a married man she was dating and wondered briefly if he'd done his usual drive by before pulling in. She shook her head, deciding not to worry about that crap on top of everything else. He came in the back door still in his bank manager clothes, and she stared, for some reason not realizing ahead of time he'd be dressed like that in the afternoon.

She figured she must look stupid in shorts and a

Lady Guadalupe and the Sno-Kone Hut T-shirt. "Give me a minute to change then we can go."

She went to the bedroom and heard him follow. He threw himself across her bed and lay with his hands behind his head. Jolene sensed dark clouds hovering over him, hanging just beneath the droopy white cotton canopy.

"That thing out Route Five?" He said loudly because she was in the bathroom.

"Yeah?" She yelled back, while washing her face, putting on some lipstick and then scraping some old mascara from underneath her eyes.

"It's official, it's going to ruin me. I can't get those lose lunatics out of my field without calling attention to the fact I own it, and the distribution people have backed out. Bad publicity they say."

She stood in the doorway, one arm up high on the doorjamb. "What do you mean?"

"That shit. That Guadalupe thing all the crazy people in this town are going wacko over. The deal is over, they backed out. It's over for me."

## Elvy Howard

Lyman Pettigrew had cursed more in the past twenty-four hours than he had in his entire life. She said, "It's impossible for Lady Guadalupe to ruin you, love doesn't ruin you." And went back to her makeup.

"How can you say such shit? How could *you*, of all people, get so caught up in this crap when you're not even Christian?"

"I told you, Lyman, if I was to be a reader I had to follow nature's way like Granny."

Lyman sighed. "I remember. You've got to be like grounded in nature, like some kind of electrical fixture, so you don't get overloaded from spirit, or some kinda crap."

"It's not crap, it's real. And I don't have to be Christian, or anything else, to recognize spirit in whatever form it takes."

"My God, Jolene, you sound like someone in a science fiction movie. *Recognize spirit,* what bullshit."

"It's not bullshit." She's stood in the doorway again, struck by something and trying to figure out what

## Lady Guadalupe and the Sno-Kone Hut

it was.

"Yes, it is total bullshit and nothing else."

"Pure spirit never ruined anyone, Lyman."

"That's what you say." He sighed again, rubbing his face with his hands.

"Have you been out there?"

"Of course I have, plenty of times. I own the land for Christ's sake."

"I mean lately since the vision moved there."

"With all the nuts from town? Are you crazy too?"

She sighed and weighed the idea of making love again. It lowered his anxiety to a level she could tolerate, and also kept her from going mad with desire.

"Hurry up and get dressed. I'm hungry." Lyman put his hands back under his head.

She saw he *was* hungry, saw the emptiness in him, but it wasn't for food, and it wasn't for her. "I think we should go down there."

"To my property? Where the distribution center

was supposed to be, but is now clogged with fruit-loops engaged in mass hysteria?"

"Yeah, that place."

"No way."

He stared at the canopy. She knew he was afraid. He should be. He couldn't hide the illegal mortgage forever, and trying to unload the property was now a long shot. "You're off the rest of the day, right?"

"That's right. I thought a little trip might be nice, get away from all the crap around here."

"Then you have to take me to Lady Guadalupe."

He sat up. "I *what*?"

"You have to take me. We have to go."

"Now don't be getting all witchy on me, Jolene."

"I'm not. I'm just telling you. Take me, or leave."

"Are you *threatening* me? Jesus Christ, I don't need this right now."

"No, I'm not threatening anything. I'm telling

Lady Guadalupe and the Sno-Kone Hut

you. Take me, or leave. Leave for good." She was still in the doorway, getting surer and clearer about what she was saying.

"What's come over you? First, you love me, and I'm so happy I don't know what to think, then all this Guadalupe shit happens, and you say get out? What the hell is going on?" He stood, agitated, with tears in his light-blue eyes.

"I'm not going to Martinsboro. I'm going to see Lady Guadalupe. You can come too, or not. It's up to you."

She knew it was merciful to do it quick, but mercy didn't make hard-loving easier.

He hung his head and didn't speak. For a second time, Jolene noticed his thinning scalp and felt such a rush of tenderness for that vulnerable pink skin she could've cried.

Instead, she stuck her feet in flip-flops, having already changed into a skirt and blouse. Neither of them moved. "Lock the back door when you leave, please," she said and left. Jolene went around Jackson at the register and didn't stop until she was in the parking lot next to her pick-up, where she hesitated.

With no sign of Lyman or the sound of his car from around back, she took a deep breath and climbed into the driver's seat. The truck started with a roar and Jolene pulled out, heading towards Route Five.

It was only a few minutes away and easy to spot, the highway lined with trucks and cars. Empty beer cans littered the area around the Sno-Kone Hut with its roof caving in. Over a field filled with broken corn stalks was a white light, visible even before she parked and Jolene noticed a great relief rolling through her.

She hadn't known she was afraid of *not* seeing Lady Guadalupe, or the Virgin, or whatever name was attached to the vision, until that moment. Getting out of the truck, she understood like everyone there, she was a beggar, too. Some were on their knees in the field. Others went from one overwhelmed individual to

Lady Guadalupe and the Sno-Kone Hut another, trying to help. Jolene slowly closed the truck's door.

The image above the field grew distinct and beautiful, and the depths of gratitude she felt was nearly frightening.

A group of men stood near a Bronco, drinking beer, watching people and laughing at the spectacle. Jolene didn't stop when one of them, Buster Tomes, called out to her. It was clear he didn't see the Lady. None in the beer-drinking group did. She didn't know why. Buster was a good guy. They'd dated a few years back. She supposed it was none of her business why and went past him to the field behind the Sno-Kone Hut.

For a moment she was unsteady under the onslaught of love – pure, sheer love – the most wondrous thing in this world and the next, and there was more love *in* and *around* everyone than she'd known. It filled her, and some kind of healing took place. A sorrow she'd lived with so long she hadn't known was there, stirred. Easing from her like a butterfly taking flight the moment she knew of it, the gentle sense memory of a mother. Some part of her cried out with a longing nearly ripping her in two, "Wait." Tears flew down her face.

"Jolene." Ethel Gunther was in front of her. "Jolene, sugar, come here." Ethel opened her arms.

Jolene walked into them, grateful someone was there. "I knew, but didn't know," she said, sobbing.

"There, there, baby." Ethel patted her back, smoothed hair from her forehead and kissed it. "Didn't none of us know, until we does. It's okay, Jolene. It's all right now. We been saved. Thanks to that good Lady up there, we don't have to let it hurt us no more." Snugging her arm around Jolene's waist, Ethel turned to face the vision.

Lady Guadalupe was no longer light. She was a huge, beautiful being suspended in the air some twenty feet over a field of dried-up cornstalks. Clutched in Ethel's arm, wiping her face with a piece of her

Lady Guadalupe and the Sno-Kone Hut

skirt and under the waves of love, it *was* okay. Jolene watched that sadness leave and cried softly for the mother who'd left such faint impressions they were nearly invisible.

Someone close by stumbled, saying, "Oh," and sat on the ground. Jolene kissed Ethel's cheek and went to the young woman, putting a hand on her shoulder. She couldn't place her right off, but it didn't matter. Jolene knew to keep talking, keep the woman's body grounded in reality, while her spirit took flight. Tears she understood, streamed down the woman's face, and like with Mateo, Jolene joined in the emotional celebration she witnessed.

Any sense of time vanished, soaking in the Lady's love, helping people as they were struck with spirit. For Jolene, alone for so long, it was like becoming part of some large organic being made up of people making contact with the vision. She knew who to help, what they needed, who to leave alone. It was the easiest thing in the world, like falling onto feathers.

## Elvy Howard

The sky was beginning to darken, and she hadn't given one thought to Lyman, the store, Jackson, nothing. Someone touched her shoulder. "Jolene?"

She was kneeling beside Evie Fisher's grandfather. It was Lyman touching her, still in his suit and tie, bewildered at everything. Jolene said, "Yeah?" She knew he couldn't see the Lady.

He bent down, hands clasped in front of him, elbows on knees. "I'm sorry I took my crap out on you."

"That's all right, Lyman. I'm fine." And she was.

"Are you seeing that thing right now?"

Jolene looked at the Lady in her billowing robes, surrounded by a glowing light so beautiful it hurt to look at after a while. Lady Guadalupe pointed in her direction and laughed silently. There was blissful joy in it. Jolene laughed back. "Yes, I am."

"Where?"

"Right where I'm looking."

Lady Guadalupe and the Sno-Kone Hut

He stared at the darkening sky, frowning.

Evie Fisher's grandfather seemed to be over the worst of it and was softly crying. Jolene patted his back, saying, "I'll be right here," and stood up. Lyman straightened too.

"She's there." Jolene pointed at the Lady who'd turned her loving gaze to another section of the crowd. She acted exactly like the proud mother of everyone there. "You have to look with your heart, Lyman."

"Maybe I don't have a heart." Sadness leaked through the words.

She laughed again. "You have a great heart."

"I'm beginning to think that might not be true. I always tried to do the right thing, but now, I don't know anymore."

His misery didn't fit with the love and joy around him. Jolene said softly, "Anytime you love, even if it's just yourself, it's a good thing, Lyman." She reached up and kissed him gently on the cheek.

He stared at her, confused at first, but she

smiled into his eyes and saw him remember all the fun they'd had the night before. How even in the middle of Lyman's dying dreams, they made love and laughed. Had fed each other scrambled eggs and sat up talking about school, their daddy's deaths, all sorts of stuff until in the middle of someone's sentence, when they both fell asleep like children, tangled in quilts and oblivious to the world. Jolene watched Lyman remember how he forgot about his property, the loan, forgot about everything but the two of them.

She was still smiling to encourage him when a shock of something like electricity went through the man and he jerked. Jolene grabbed hold of him so he wouldn't fall and felt the faint, tingly aftereffects of lingering spirit.

Lyman looked up, saying loudly, "Oh my God," and fell to his knees. The Lady was laughing in their direction, probably at him this time, and Jolene knelt beside Lyman like she'd done with so many others that day.

Lady Guadalupe and the Sno-Kone Hut

It was fully dark before he came back to himself. Lyman was the type who left. His kind were scattered around, people struck down and unable to hear anything, see anything, say anything, but still needing the comfort of another person beside them. Jolene stayed next to him and continued to speak gently to Evie Fisher's grandfather until the old man was ready to get up and go home.

The Lady glowed softly in the warm night, growing less distinct and the crowd had thinned.

Jolene was filled with peace, and she startled when Lyman spoke. "She's still there." He was looking up.

"Yes, she is." Jolene patted his shoulder.

Lyman stared at Lady Guadalupe for a while, soaking in her love and then looked at his property, like seeing it for the first time. He took a deep, deep breath. "If I'm lucky, I'll end up paying for this place the rest of my life, won't I?"

"So what?"

He glanced at her. "So what?" He was too tired to get riled, too worn out from wherever he'd been.

"Yeah, so what? What else did you have to do with your life, you fool, but live it?" Jolene had been smiling for a long time. She was still smiling.

It took a moment, but finally, he got it. Lyman started with a snicker, little more than, "huh," then said, "You're right. What in hell else did I have to do?" He shrugged and began laughing for real. Soon he was laughing so hard, as was Jolene, they ended up rolling on the ground, clutching their sides. Jolene knew her banker could have cared less about his suit, people seeing them together, or any of the crap he used to haul around.

"You ready to go home, Lyman?" Jolene said, wiping her eyes when their laughter slowed to the point she could speak.

"Home? Where's that?" He was still chuckling.

"Down by the river," she said, suddenly shy and catching her breath.

Lady Guadalupe and the Sno-Kone Hut

He sat up and inhaled deeply. With a sigh, Lyman let the air escape his lungs. Brushing off his pants legs, he stood and reached a hand to Jolene.

Pulling her to him, he kissed her, right in front of the fading Lady Guadalupe and half the town. It was a wonderful kiss, his best yet. Jolene could hardly wait to get him home. He picked a leaf, or something, from her hair. "Yes, is the answer to your question. Yes, I'm ready to go home." And he kissed her again.

## Author's Note

When I was a child, Life Magazine did an article on the Melungeons. They existed in close-knit groups, in Appalachia, and what fascinated me the most was, no one knew where they came from.

I was consumed with curiosity when learning the first European settlers making it as far west as the Appalachians, found English speaking, odd-looking people already settled in the area and began calling them Melungeons. No one is entirely sure the name's origins. Some had tight, curly, coarse hair; some had light, almost straight, fine hair. Their skin color was a mixed bag, with some of them swarthy, others fair. Some had light eyes, and others were dark enough to pass for Native, or African Americans.

The Melungeons insisted they were Portuguese mixed with Native American tribes. They had good reason to distance themselves from any association with African Americans, as slavery, civil war, and Jim Crow laws threatened their freedom. Mostly, they were left to their own ways, and were viewed with suspicion by neighboring whites.

DNA testing has finally solved the centuries-old question, and determined the Melungeon line came from two people (I know—amazing), a Northern European female and a sub-Saharan African male in the 1600s. In those days there was no slavery, and they most likely were indentured servants running from servitude. The clan these two people started did mix with various native and non-native peoples while continuing their westward migration before encroaching civilization finally caught up with them.

In the same way, Jolene's past catches up with her, and like the brave and fiercely independent people she came from, she faces it head on.

About the Author

Elvy Howard lives in Midlothian, Virginia with her husband, two dogs, and one cat, where she's frequently visited by her four gorgeous, talented, and highly above-average grandchildren.

Elvy would love to hear from you. Visit her at Elvy-Howard.com, or better, email her at elvy@elvyhoward.com

Made in the USA
Lexington, KY
21 September 2018

# LIZZIE

## By May Justus

First published in 1944

This unabridged version has updated grammar and spelling.

© 2019 Jenny Phillips

www.thegoodandthebeautiful.com

Cover illustration by

Ecaterina Leascenco and Christine Chisholm

Cover design by Elle Staples

Illustrations by Christine Chisholm